Charles Dickens

A Tale of Two Cities

雙城記

Adaptation and activities by Janet Borsbey and Ruth Swan
Illustrated by Giacomo Garelli

The Commercial Press

Contents 目錄

故事錄音開始和結束的標記

start ▶ stop ■

MAIN CHARACTERS

Doctor Alexandre Manette

Mr Jarvis Lorry

Lucie Manette

Sydney Carton

Charles Darnay

Madame Thérèse Defarge

Ernest Defarge

Miss Pross

Jerry Cruncher

Setting the Scene

1 Read the introduction to *A Tale of Two Cities*. Decide which answer – A, B, C or D best fits each gap.

Introduction

A Tales of Two Cities (**1**)________ first published in 1859. It was not originally published as a novel; it was (**2**)________ divided into weekly instalments in a magazine, *All the Year Round*. The two cities in the (**3**)________ are Paris and London, and the story is set at the time of the French Revolution. The threat of revolution and social change was in the air all (**4**)________ Europe at the time, and the after-effects of both the French and the American Revolutions were being felt. Dickens thought that there was a chance that revolution would come to Britain, too.

Critics today consider that Dickens was (**5**)________ great changes in his own life by writing about change in society: Dickens had separated from his wife the year before, after a long, unhappy (**6**)________. Furthermore, he had left his publishers after a disagreement, and *All the Year Round* was a new publication that he had started. *A Tale of Two Cities* (**7**)________ one of Dickens most popular novels and has been adapted for television, theatre, cinema and radio many times.

	A	B	C	D
1	☐ had	☐ was	☐ is	☐ were
2	☐ sincerely	☐ properly	☐ actually	☐ lovely
3	☐ title	☐ page	☐ headline	☐ top
4	☐ that	☐ by	☐ in	☐ over
5	☐ having	☐ viewing	☐ seeing	☐ reflecting
6	☐ wedding	☐ marriage	☐ relation	☐ engagement
7	☐ remains	☐ stays	☐ lasts	☐ takes

Vocabulary

2 Reporting Verbs. Solve these anagrams to find verbs we can use to report speech. Then fill the gaps to complete the sentences with the Past Simple of the verbs.

1	sak	'How far exactly is it?' *asked* the child.
2	masrce	'Help!' the old man __________ .
3	lyper	'Why?' she __________ .
4	erwnas	'Because it's time,' the girl __________ .
5	ryc	'Ouch! That hurts!' he __________ .
6	ousth	'Look out!' they __________ . 'There's a car!
7	eirwphs	'Shh! They'll hear us,' the small boy __________ .

The Story

3 In *A Tale of Two Cities*, a number of different places are mentioned, including the following:

- Tellson's Bank
- The Port of Dover
- The prison at La Force
- The Bastille
- The Old Bailey Court
- The George Hotel in Dover
- The prison at the Abbaye
- A café in Saint Antoine, Paris

What predictions can you make about the story from the names of these places?

4 The first chapter of *A Tale of Two Cities* is called *Recalled to Life*. Tick the words you expect to read. Then read and check.

death	☐	robbery	☐
funeral	☐	passenger	☐
young	☐	king	☐
elderly	☐	punishment	☐
prisoner	☐	crime	☐
nervous	☐	gun	☐

Chapter One

Recalled to Life

▶ 2 It was the best of times, it was the worst of times, it was the age of wisdom, it was the age of stupidity, it was the season of Light, it was the season of Darkness, it was the spring of hope, it was the winter of despair, we had everything to look forward to, we had nothing to look forward to, we were all going directly to Heaven, we were all going directly the other way – in short, it was a time much like today.

A king with a large chin and a queen with a plain face ruled England. A king with a large chin and a queen with a pretty face ruled France. Nothing had changed and nothing would change. Things would be this way forever. King George III of England and his Queen Charlotte Sophia were sure of that. King Louis XIV and his Queen Marie Antoinette were sure of that, too. It was the year 1775.

Times were hard and the people were quietly angry. Poor people *had* nothing and *were* nothing. Rich people had *everything* and were *everything*. There was justice, but justice was cruel. In France, the people were afraid: even less serious crimes were punished with terrible punishments.

In England, the people were afraid, too. Robbery and murder were common, so no-one felt there was justice. The punishments didn't seem to match the crimes: the courts didn't seem to be able to tell the difference between a thief and a murderer.

Our story starts in England, on a dark, rainy Friday night in late November, as the mail coach[1] was making its way to the port of Dover. It was cold and wet; the road was muddy and the horses were tired. The coach was getting heavier and heavier with the mud and now the hill was too much for them. The driver was nervous and so were the passengers: robberies were common and the Dover road was a favourite place for robbers to wait. The three passengers had no choice. They got out and began to walk up the hill in the mist and the rain, beside the coach. The mail guard looked down at his gun to check it was there.

'Listen, Joe. Can you hear that?' called the driver.

'I can't hear anything, Tom.'

'It's a horse, I'm sure it is. Get your gun and look out.'

The driver stopped the coach and the guard picked up his gun and listened. Yes, there it was! He could hear the sound of a horse in the distance and it was getting closer. 'Stop! Who's there? Stop or I'll shoot!'

'I'm looking for a passenger,' said a voice from the mist.

'What passenger?'

'Mr Jarvis Lorry.'

'That's me,' said one of the passengers. 'Is that you Jerry? What's the matter?'

'I've got a message from Tellson's Bank for you.'

'Come forward, then,' said the guard, with his finger on his gun,

1. coach: 老式四輪大馬車（現用於官方或皇家典禮中）

'but keep your hands where I can see them.'

The passengers hid their watches and valuable things deep inside their coats. The horse and rider came out of the mist, both were covered from head to foot in mud. The rider got off and handed Mr Lorry a piece of paper. Mr Lorry thanked him and read:

Wait at Dover for the young lady.

'Well Jerry, tell them that my answer is *Recalled to life*.'

'That's a very strange answer, sir.'

'Maybe it is, but when they hear that, they'll know that the answer is from *me* and from no-one else. Good night.'

The coach slowly moved on again and Jerry watched until it disappeared in the mist. '*Recalled to life*. What kind of answer is that? Very strange. Very strange. No, Jerry, he can't know, but that wouldn't suit *my* sort of work!' he said to himself.

Meanwhile, the coach moved on and Mr Lorry became lost in his dreams. He was on his way to dig someone out of a grave[1]. But which of the ghostly faces that he saw in his dreams was the face of the buried person? Proud, sad, angry faces, but always the face of a man of about forty-five. Tired, pale and thin, and with every hair on his head completely white. 'Buried? How long?' Mr Lorry repeatedly asked this ghost.

The answer was always the same 'Eighteen years. Eighteen years.'

'Shall I bring her to you?' asked Mr Lorry.

Here, the answers were often different, sometimes his ghost was crying, 'No! It's too soon.' sometimes impatient, 'Take me to her,' or sometimes confused, 'I don't know her, I don't understand.'

And when the imaginary conversation finished, Mr Lorry would start to dig, dig and dig.

1. grave: 墳墓

The words 'eighteen years' were still in his ears when he woke up. However, the shadows of the ghostly face faded away with the rising sun.

◈◈◈

The mail coach finally arrived in Dover and stopped at The George Hotel. By this time, there was only one remaining passenger and he was wrapped up from head to toe to keep warm. He was shown to his room and the staff eagerly waited for him to re-appear, to see what their new guest looked like. He washed and changed and went down to breakfast. Mr Lorry was about sixty years old. He was dressed in a formal brown suit that was a little worn, but very well-kept. He had bright eyes and a healthy colour in his cheeks and, though his face was lined, it wasn't from worry. He sat still by the fire and waited patiently for his meal but, with the effects of the warmth from the fire and the long journey, Mr Lorry dropped off to sleep.

The noise of his breakfast arriving woke him and he said to the waiter, 'Please get a room ready for a young lady. She could arrive at any time today. She might ask for Mr Jarvis Lorry, she might ask for a gentleman from Tellson's Bank. Please let me know when she gets here.'

Late in the evening, while Mr Lorry was finishing his dinner, he heard the sound of wheels, on the road outside. The sound stopped at the hotel, 'This is the young lady!' he said to himself.

Sure enough, the waiter came to tell him that Miss Manette had arrived from London and wanted to see the gentleman from Tellson's Bank as soon as possible.

Miss Manette was still wearing her travelling coat and holding her hat, when Mr Lorry went into her sitting room. She was a pretty young lady, about seventeen years old and with blonde hair and blue eyes. For a tiny moment, he thought she looked like the child that he had once held in his arms, protecting her from the wind and rain, while crossing the Channel from France. Then the thought disappeared from his mind and he kissed her hand.

'Please sit down,' she said.

Her voice was clear and pleasant and you could only just tell that she was French, not English. 'I received a letter saying something about a discovery about my poor father. My long dead father, who I never saw. The letter mentioned going to Paris but, as I am alone in the world, I asked if I could go with a gentleman from Tellson's to protect me and help me.'

'Myself, Miss.'

'Yes, so they sent a message to you, to ask if you would be kind enough to wait for me. They said you would tell me some news and that some of it might be surprising to me. What news have you got for me? I'm very interested to know.'

'It is difficult to know where to begin. I am a man of business and my story concerns one of our customers in France. It was twenty years ago and he was a French gentleman and a Doctor, like your father. Also like your father, he was from Beauvais and was well-respected in Paris. At that time, I was working in our French bank and I had been working there for many years. The doctor married an English lady and ...'

'But this is my father's story, sir. Do I know you? I'm beginning to

think I do. My mother only lived a few years after my father died. Was it you who brought me to England? I'm almost sure it was. Please tell me.'

'Yes, it was me, and Tellson's Bank have been looking after you ever since. But this isn't the whole of my story. What if your father, Doctor Manette, didn't die when you think he did? What if he had just disappeared? What if he had been taken away? Perhaps no-one knew where to, although it would have been easy to guess. What if his wife had asked and asked and asked for help to find him? If she had asked everyone possible, even the king and queen, but no-one told her? In that case, my story wouldn't be your father's story, but the story of my doctor from Beauvais.'

'Please tell me more. I'm a little afraid, but I have to know the truth.'

'Good. You're a brave young lady and you need to be. I'll go on. His wife had a baby. Yes, a girl. Then, two years later, his wife died, I believe broken-hearted, after never stopping to search for him. However, she hadn't wanted her child to suffer as she had suffered, so she let the girl believe both parents were dead. Now, this story *does* become your father's story and I have to tell you, that he has been found. He has another name, but he's alive. He has been in prison all these years, not dead as you were told. He has changed a lot and he's no longer the man he once was but, Miss Manette, the truth is he really *is* alive. He has been taken to the house of an old servant in Paris and we're going to go there to see him. This is a secret mission, Miss. We mustn't let anyone know his true identity or he will be in terrible danger. My job is to identify him, if I can, and yours is to look after him and bring him back to health.'

Miss Manette's face went white. She gripped Mr Lorry's hand and began to faint. 'I'm going to see his ghost, not him. His ghost!'

Mr Lorry called for help and immediately a large, wild-looking woman ran into the room and pushed him back against the wall. She was very red in the face and had a strange hat on her head. Mr Lorry wasn't even sure if she was a woman or a man, she was so strong.

'What have you done, you in brown? Couldn't you tell her what you had to without frightening her to death? Do you call that being a banker?'

Mr Lorry was confused and didn't really know how to answer, but then, shouting at the servants, the wild woman went on, 'Don't just stand there you lazy lot. Go and fetch some water for my young lady!'

Despite his confusion, Mr Lorry was impressed by the woman's care and attention for Miss Manette. 'I very much hope you'll be coming to France with Miss Manette, Madam,' he said.

'If nature had intended me to go across salt water, do you think I would have been born on an island?'

Mr Lorry thought about this for a moment and, not really knowing how to answer this question either, he decided it would be better to leave. He left the room, still thinking about it. ■

Stop & Check

1 Put these nine events into the order they appear in Chapter One.

1 ☐ He handed over a message to one of the travellers, a Mr Lorry.
2 ☐ Miss Manette felt faint and a lady with a red face looked after her.
3 ☐ Mr Lorry asked a servant there to tell him as soon as a lady called Miss Manette arrived.
4 ☐ Mr Lorry then gave a message for the man to take to Tellson's Bank.
5 ☐ Mr Lorry told her that her father was still alive.
6 ☐ The coach finally arrived at The George Hotel in Dover.
7 ☐ The mail coach was travelling to Dover.
8 ☐ A man on a horse stopped the coach.
9 ☐ When the lady arrived, she asked to speak to Mr Lorry immediately.

Vocabulary

2 Look again at the first page of Chapter One. Find words that mean the same as the words/phrases below. The words are in the same order in the text.

1 wait for excitedly ____________________
2 governed ____________________
3 certain ____________________
4 difficult ____________________
5 silently ____________________
6 frightened ____________________
7 horrible ____________________
8 killing ____________________
9 often happened ____________________

Vocabulary & Writing

3a Complete the sentences by forming a noun from the adjectives given.

1 It was the season of *darkness*, but also the season of *light*. dark, light
2 It was the age of ________, but also the age of ________. wise, stupid
3 It was the spring of ________, it was the winter of ________. hopeful, despairing
4 There was a ________ system, but it was known for its ________. just, cruel
5 People in Paris and in London suffered in ________. poor
6 The courts didn't seem to be able to tell the ________ between a thief and a murderer. different
7 ________ is important to this mission. secret
8 You must bring your father back to ________. healthy

3b Choose one of the following things to do. Write a paragraph about it.

a wise thing to do • a stupid thing to do
a just thing to do • a healthy thing to do

Speaking

4 Discuss the following questions in pairs.

1 Have you ever travelled on horseback or in a horse-drawn vehicle? What was it like?
2 Imagine travelling by coach in November 1775. What might the dangers be?
3 Have you ever travelled by boat? What was it like?
4 Imagine travelling by sea in November 1775. What might the dangers be?
5 Is there a capital city in the world that you would like to visit?
6 Is there a means of transport that you have never tried, but would like to try?

5 **Use of English. Complete the second sentence so that it has a similar meaning to the first sentence, using the word given. Do not change the word given. You must use between two and five words, including the word given.**

1 She had never been to Paris before.
FIRST
It .... she had ever been to Paris.

2 It was only because the coach had stopped that the messenger caught them.
NEVER
If the coach hadn't stopped .... caught them.

3 Mr Lorry advised Miss Manette to look after her father.
WERE
'If .... look after your father,' Mr Lorry said.

4 The horses couldn't pull the coach up the hill because it was too steep.
MUCH
The hill .... for the horses.

5 I wish I had known that my father was alive!
ONLY
If .... that my father was alive.

6 'She has arrived from London,' said the waiter to him.
TOLD
The waiter .... arrived from London.

7 They decided to stay in the hotel, because there was a chance of rain.
CASE
They decided to stay in the hotel .... rained.

8 'I'd prefer to get a boat in the morning.'
RATHER
I .... in the morning.

Writing

6 Imagine you are Lucie Manette. Write a diary entry for the evening after your conversation with Mr Lorry.

- Explain exactly what happened when you arrived at the hotel.
- Describe Mr Lorry.
- Explain what Mr Lorry said to you.
- Say how you felt and how you're feeling now.

BEFORE-READING ACTIVITY

Vocabulary & Speaking

7a Are these adjectives from Chapter Two positive (P), negative (N) or both (B)? Tick the boxes.

	P	N	B
1 narrow	☐	☐	☐
2 strong	☐	☐	☐
3 curly	☐	☐	☐
4 faint	☐	☐	☐
5 round	☐	☐	☐
6 steady	☐	☐	☐
7 elderly	☐	☐	☐
8 poor	☐	☐	☐
9 steep	☐	☐	☐
10 poisonous	☐	☐	☐

7b Talk in pairs. In Chapter Two, Lucie Manette meets her father for the first time. Where do you think she finds him? What do you think he's like?

Chapter Two

The Café, the Three Men Called Jacques and the Lonely Shoemaker

▶ 3 A large barrel[1] of wine had fallen off the wine cart and broken into pieces, just outside the café. Everyone had heard the noise, or seen the barrel fall and, all along the street, people had stopped what they were doing to run and save the wine. Some people simply put their two hands together, filled them with wine and drank. Some people came running up with cups and filled them from the steady red river. Others collected the wood from the broken barrel. Everyone was happy and laughing. Slowly, as the wine disappeared, it left the ground of that narrow street in Saint Antoine, in Paris, stained a deep, blood red colour. Then, as soon as the wine had disappeared the people returned to the hard, cold reality of their daily lives; lives of hunger, poverty and illness; working all the time, but for what?

The owner of the café had stood on the corner, outside his shop and watched the scene. 'It's nothing to do with me,' he said, not seeming at all worried. 'It's the cart driver's fault, he can bring me another barrel.'

The owner was a strong-looking man of about thirty and he clearly didn't feel the cold because, although it was a freezing cold day, he wasn't wearing a coat and his shirt sleeves were rolled up, too. Nor did a hat cover his dark, curly hair. He had a good, kind face but

1. barrel: 桶

it was difficult to tell from his expression or from his eyes what he was thinking.

Madame Defarge, his wife, was sitting behind the counter when he came in. She was a rather round woman of about his own age. She had fat hands and, on them, she wore several large rings. She had a strong, steady expression on her face and you could see she was the type of woman who noticed everything that went on around her. Unlike Monsieur Defarge, she *did* feel the cold and she was wrapped up from head to toe in very warm clothing. She was knitting, as usual, and her fingers moved quickly.

She put her work down for a moment when her husband came in, and signalled to him to look around and see if any new customers had arrived. He looked around and saw an elderly gentleman and a young lady that he didn't recognise, sitting at a table in a corner. The gentleman looked at him, as if to say, 'That's the man we want'. The other people in the room were all familiar to him; some were playing cards and some were just chatting. He pretended not to notice the two new visitors and went to talk to three of his customers in another part of the room.

'How are things, Jacques[1]?' said one of the three to Monsieur Defarge.'

'All's well, Jacques,' Monsieur Defarge replied.

Then, the second man spoke. 'Thing's aren't so well for those poor people out there, though, are they Jacques?'

'That's very true, Jacques, very true,' Monsieur Defarge answered.

At this second use of the name *Jacques*, Madame Defarge looked up and raised an eyebrow.

1. Jacques: 雅克
在法國大革命期間，很多人都使用這個名字。他們互相不知道對方的真實身份，但通常戴着一頂紅帽子，來顯示自己是革命的一份子。

The third man now had his say, 'Yes, their lives are terribly hard, they work and work and work but have nothing to eat. Am I right, Jacques?'

'Yes, you're right, Jacques, you are.'

At this *third* mention of the name *Jacques*, Madame Defarge put down her knitting, raised her eyebrow even more and moved a little in her chair.

'My wife, gentlemen. My wife.'

The three men took off their red caps and greeted her. She bent her head slightly, and then continued with her knitting.

'Gentlemen,' continued Monsieur Defarge, 'the room you were asking about is on the fifth floor, but now I remember, one of you has already been there, so he can show you the way.'

The three Jacques paid their bill and left the café. Monsieur Defarge turned his attention to the elderly man and the young lady.

'May I have a word,' asked the elderly man.

'Of course, sir,' replied Monsieur Defarge.

The two men spoke for a very short time and Monsieur Defarge was clearly very interested. Soon, the elderly man signalled to the young lady to follow him with Monsieur Defarge and the three left the café. Madame Defarge's quick fingers carried on knitting. She saw nothing.

'Come with me. Come with me,' said Monsieur Defarge. 'I'll take you to him. Come with me.'

Mr Jarvis Lorry, Miss Manette and Monsieur Defarge crossed a dirty, smelly, dark square and went into a dirty, smelly, dark building. 'Be careful, the stairs are steep,' said Monsieur Defarge. There was anger in his voice.

'Is he alone?' whispered Mr Lorry. 'Has he changed much?'

'Changed? He is the same as he was when I first saw him: when they brought him to me here and warned me to be careful.'

A staircase, in a building in such as this, in any large city would be terrible today, but *then* it was so much worse. It was a great, high building, home to many hundreds. Each door that opened onto the shared staircase had its own collection of rubbish outside. This would have polluted the air in any case, yet added to it was the air of extreme poverty[1]. The way to his room lay through this poisonous atmosphere up the steep, dark staircase.

Then, finally, they got to the top of the main staircase, but Mr Lorry cried in horror as he realised that this was just the bottom of an upper staircase. Monsieur Defarge pulled a key from his pocket.

'Is the door locked, my friend?' he asked.

'I think it is necessary; he has lived so long alone that he would be frightened, perhaps even die, if the door was left open.'

They went up slowly and softly and were soon at the top. There was only one door, but there were some small holes in the wall of the room. Looking through the wall were the three Jacques from the café.

'Is Monsieur Manette a *show* for these people?' said Mr Lorry, horrified.

'I show him to some people: men who share my opinions. But only if I think it will do them good.' Monsieur Defarge put the key into the lock and began to turn it.

Miss Manette looked faint and Mr Lorry put his arm around her to hold her up.

1. poverty: 貧窮、貧困

'I'm afraid! Afraid of my father!' she said.

Monsieur Defarge opened the door wide and walked into the small, dark room. There, by the window, where Monsieur Defarge stood looking at him, a white-haired man sat on a low bench, leaning forward, very busily making shoes.

'Good morning,' said Monsieur Defarge. 'You're working hard, I see.'

'Good morning, yes. I'm working.'

The man's voice was faint and terrible; not because he was physically weak, although it was clear he had been in prison for a long time. It was terrible, because its faintness came from lack of use. It was like the last, sad echo[1] of a sound made long ago: like a voice from under the ground.

The man continued with his work. Mr Lorry opened the door a little more and light fell on an unfinished shoe, some small pieces of leather on the floor and on the bench and some simple tools. The man had a short white beard, a thin face and very bright eyes. He looked up as Mr Lorry came closer to him, but showed no surprise.

'You have a visitor, you see,' said Monsieur Defarge. 'Tell him about your shoe.'

'It is a lady's shoe. A young lady's walking shoe.' There was a touch of pride in his voice.

'And the maker's name is?' asked Defarge.

'One Hundred and Five, North Tower.' With a tired sound, not quite a sigh, he bent over his work again.

'I don't think you were always a shoemaker,' said Mr Lorry, looking steadily at him.

1. echo: 回聲、回響

'No, no. I think. I asked to ... I ... I learnt it here,' he said. His eyes wandered slowly away.

'Doctor Manette, don't you remember me at all?' asked Mr Lorry, still looking steadily at him.

The shoe dropped to the ground. As the prisoner of many years sat looking at Mr Lorry and at Defarge, some faint expression[1] of recognition forced itself through the black mist and then was gone. The expression on his face was the same as that of the young lady who had come into the room and was standing with her arms held out towards him. The expression was so exactly repeated, that it seemed as though it had passed like a moving light from his face to hers. She stood, like a spirit, beside him, and he bent over his work. Eventually, his eyes saw her dress. He looked up and saw her long golden hair. Slowly he put out his hand and touched her curls. He sighed, looked down and continued with his work.

But not for long. He soon put down his work, looked at her again, put his hand to his neck and took off a piece of black string with a piece of cotton attached to it. He opened this, carefully, and pulled out one or two long golden hairs, which he had kept for many years.

'How can this be? When they took me to the North Tower, they found these hairs on my sleeve. Are they yours? They can't be. You are too young. Yet your hair and your voice are like hers.'

'My mother's hair, my mother's voice, though she is long dead. Your pain is over, dear father,' she cried, holding him in her arms.

They stayed like that for so long that, eventually, worn out, he fell asleep.

1. expression: 表情

'We must leave Paris, at once,' said Miss Manette to her companions. 'I will stay with him, while you arrange things.'

It was very near the end of the day, so Monsieur Defarge and Mr Lorry agreed. There was a coach and horses to be found, travelling papers to arrange, clothes, food and drink to be prepared. At last, when all had been done, they came for Doctor Manette. Nobody could be sure if he knew he was free. When they spoke to him, there was always an air of confusion in his voice. The only sign of recognition he gave was when his daughter spoke; his head always turned to look for her. The only thing he repeated as they took him carefully down the poisonous staircase was 'One Hundred and Five, North Tower'.

There was no crowd in the street, and the silence was almost unnatural. Only one person could be seen, and that was Madame Defarge, who stood near the door, knitting, and saw nothing.

The prisoner had got into the coach and his daughter had followed, when Mr Lorry heard him ask for his shoemaking tools. Madame Defarge called to her husband that she would get them. She quickly brought them down, gave them to the old man, and went back to the door, knitting, seeing nothing.

Seconds later, the coach departed. Mr Jarvis Lorry sat till dawn, opposite the buried man who had been dug out from his grave, and wondering whether Doctor Manette knew he had been *recalled to life*, or whether he even wanted it. ■

Stop & Check

1 Who did these things happen to, or who did these things in Chapter Two?

Choose from:

A Lucie
B Madame Defarge
C Doctor Manette
D Mr Lorry

Which person:

1 ☐ wore lots of clothes because she often felt cold?
2 ☐ was older and sat in the café with Lucie?
3 ☐ spent her time knitting?
4 ☐ was shocked when he realised a man's room was locked?
5 ☐ was surprised when he saw people looking at another person?
6 ☐ was afraid of meeting her father?
7 ☐ made shoes?
8 ☐ used to live in a tower?
9 ☐ was surprised that someone didn't remember him from the past?
10 ☐ had kept some golden hairs for many years?
11 ☐ asked for some tools?
12 ☐ pretended to see nothing?

2 Look again at the first page of Chapter Two and answer the questions.

1 What colour was the wine?

____

2 Why do you think people took the wood?

____

3 How does Dickens describe people's daily lives?

____

4 How do you think the colour of the wine might be important for the rest of the story?

____

Vocabulary

3 Wordsearch. There are nine abstract nouns from Chapter Two in this wordsearch. Find them and put them into the gaps in the sentences below.

1 The people returned to the hard, cold r________ of their daily lives. (7 letters)
2 'It's the cart driver's f________, he can bring me another barrel.' (5 letters)
3 'Be careful, the stairs are steep.' There was a________ in his voice. (5 letters)
4 Added to it was the air of extreme p________. (7 letters)
5 The way to his room lay through this poisonous a________. (10 letters)
6 Mr Lorry came closer to him, but showed no s________. (8 letters)
7 There was a touch of p________ in his voice. (5 letters)
8 Some faint expression of r________ forced itself through the black mist. (11 letters)
9 There was always an air of c________ in his voice. (9 letters)

R	U	K	D	A	F	F	P	I	N	S
L	E	A	N	G	E	R	O	E	E	U
F	O	C	C	F	Y	O	V	C	U	R
A	T	M	O	S	P	H	E	R	E	P
U	A	R	N	G	E	N	R	H	O	R
L	A	R	F	E	N	L	T	S	E	I
T	P	L	U	O	E	I	Y	J	A	S
V	N	R	S	D	N	R	T	A	U	E
E	H	U	I	R	E	A	L	I	T	Y
R	T	E	O	D	T	A	O	C	O	N
D	M	P	N	T	E	T	L	E	A	N

Writing for First

4a **Make a note of all the problems with the building where Doctor Manette was living.**

4b **Write a letter of <u>complaint</u> to your local newspaper. Explain what the problems with the building are and say what you think should be done about them. Write 120-180 words.**

Speaking for First

5 **Work in pairs to discuss the questions below.**

1 Would you rather live in the city or the countryside?

2 Do you think life in the countryside is healthier than life in the city?

3 What type of facilities are available to people in a town rather than the countryside?

4 Are there any problems with poor accommodation in your city? If so, what would you do about them?

Vocabulary

6 Which of these words is the odd one out? Write your reasons below.

1 ☐ barrel ☐ jar ☐ bottle ☐ glass

____

2 ☐ elderly ☐ old ☐ ancient ☐ young

____

3 ☐ icy ☐ freezing ☐ cold ☐ warm

____

4 ☐ shoe ☐ boot ☐ cap ☐ sandal

____

5 ☐ toe ☐ finger ☐ arm ☐ hand

____

BEFORE-READING ACTIVITY

Listening & Speaking

7a Tick ✓ the adjectives you think might be used when describing the headquarters of a bank. Explain your answers to your partner.

1 ☐ steel
2 ☐ wooden
3 ☐ plastic
4 ☐ large
5 ☐ dark
6 ☐ old-fashioned
7 ☐ small
8 ☐ ugly
9 ☐ spacious
10 ☐ beautiful
11 ☐ comfortable
12 ☐ old
13 ☐ damp
14 ☐ modern

▶ 4 **7b Listen to the description of Tellson's Bank in London from the beginning of Chapter Three. Underline the adjectives you hear in the text. Now read the first few lines of Chapter Three and check your answers.**

Chapter Three

The Blue Flies Buzz, Buzz, Buzz

▶ 4 Tellson's Bank was an old-fashioned place, even in the year 1780. It was very small, very dark, very ugly and very uncomfortable, but it was also old-fashioned in that the owners were actually proud of its size, proud of its darkness, proud of its ugliness and proud of its lack of comfort. Tellson's considered itself to be perfect.

Customers entered this miserable place through an old door, where they met two of the oldest men in business. Customers' money came out of, or went into, old wooden drawers. Their bank notes smelt old and damp, as did their family papers, which were stored upstairs and were looked at by criminals who had been executed[1]: the criminals' heads were often placed on the city gates outside the bank. This was quite right, since Tellson's was responsible for putting some of them to death: those who had committed crimes against money.

When a young man joined Tellson's, he was taken into the building and hidden away until he was old. They kept him in a dark place, like a cheese, until he had the full Tellson taste. Only then was he allowed to be seen.

Outside Tellson's stood the only sign of life. He was always there, this ugly, monkey-like man, whose name was Jerry Cruncher, unless he was replaced by his ugly twelve-year-old son, young Jerry Cruncher. Jerry Cruncher, the father, took messages and acted as

1. executed: 處決了

a bodyguard. His boots were always muddy and he had a habit of throwing them at his wife when she prayed: he had always been afraid of her praying. There were things the son didn't understand about the father: where did he go at night? And why were his fingers always stained brown?

This particular morning, Mr Jerry Cruncher and young Jerry Cruncher, who were always *very* respectful to the gentlemen at Tellson's, were in position outside the bank by a quarter to nine. It didn't take long for the first job of the day to appear.

'Do you know the Old Bailey?' said one of the oldest bankers.

'Ye-es, sir,' said Mr Cruncher. 'I do know the courts at the Old Bailey: only a very little. I'm an honest man, sir.'

'Good. Show the doorman at the Old Bailey this note for Mr Lorry. He'll then let you in.'

'In, sir?' Mr Cruncher's eyes seemed a little concerned.

'Into the court. Mr Lorry might want to send a message. Wait, until he calls you.'

'What's the trial, sir? Another thief?'

'No, a traitor[1]!'

'Treason[2]? That's a horrible punishment.'

'That's the law! Take my advice: take care of your health and let the law take care of itself.'

Jerry took the letter and set off for the Old Bailey, the law court from which pale travellers went off on their short journey to Tyburn, the place where they hanged prisoners these days, only two and a half miles away. Mr Cruncher gave his message to the doorman. The door was well-guarded: people always paid well to get in. After a few short

1. traitor: 叛徒
2. Treason: 叛國罪

minutes, having attracted Mr Lorry's attention, he was sitting in the court, waiting.

The judge came into the court and looked around. Lawyers and the people in the public seats stopped talking. Everyone looked towards an area in the court, known as the dock. It was empty. Then, there was movement. The prisoner was brought into the dock. Every human breath in the court rolled at him like a sea. Faces looked around corners to catch sight of him; people in the public seats stood up so they could get a better view of him; people on the floor of the courtroom used chairs, other people's shoulders, shelves, anything, just so that they could see him.

They were staring at a young man of about twenty-five. He was tall and good-looking with skin brown from the sun and dark eyes. He was a young gentleman, although he was dressed in plain, dark clothes. His hair was tied back. The young man looked calmly around and looked at the judge with respect.

'Silence in the court!' called an officer, who reminded everyone that Charles Darnay had yesterday declared himself *Not Guilty* of treason against the King of England. He denied, said the officer with a tone of disbelief, helping King Louis of France by giving information about British plans for Canada and North America.

The accused, who was (and who knew he was) being hanged in the minds of everybody there, paid quiet attention to the opening of his trial. At one point, light caught the mirror above his head and this made the prisoner turn his head away. His eyes fell on two people sitting near to the Judge's bench and his face changed so much that all eyes in the court turned to look at the people he had seen.

They saw two people, a young lady who could not have been older than twenty and a gentleman who was obviously her father; his hair was pure white and his face was thoughtful. When he looked at his daughter, his face became handsome, not old and broken.

The daughter was sitting close to her father and it was clear that she felt only pity for the prisoner.

There was a whisper in the court, 'Who are they?' and everyone, including Jerry, tried to hear the answer as it was passed back from person to person.

'Witnesses – against the prisoner!'

The prosecutor[1] rose to his feet to begin the prosecution. He told the jury[2] that the prosecution would present Proof that Darnay was Guilty of the terrible Crime of Treason; that a Patriot[3] would give Evidence; that a Servant would give Evidence; that there were two important Witnesses, and that the only possible Sentence (if innocent people and their children were to be able to sleep safely in their beds at night) was Death.

When the prosecutor sat down, there was a buzz in the court, like the sound of a cloud of blue flies buzzing around the prisoner's head. Mr Cruncher's brown fingers were in his mouth.

The first witness in the court was John Barsad, the patriot. He stated that he was giving evidence because he loved his country and that Charles Darnay was a traitor. The defence lawyer started with his questions. Had Barsad ever been a spy[4] himself? No, no! Had he ever been in prison? No, no! What about a debtors' prison? Well, yes. And had he ever borrowed money from Charles Darnay? Yes. And had he paid the money back? Well, no.

1. prosecutor: 檢察官
2. jury: 陪審團
3. Patriot: 愛國者
4. spy: 間諜

Then came the honest servant, Roger Cly. He had started working for the prisoner, Charles Darnay, four years ago. He had watched the prisoner carefully. He loved his country and he couldn't bear the idea of a traitor. He had never been suspected of stealing a silver teapot. No, he hadn't stolen a silver bowl – the bowl hadn't been made of silver.

The blue flies buzzed again, and the prosecutor called Mr Lorry, 'Did you travel on the mail coach one Friday night in November, 1775?'

'I did.'

'Did you see this man,' the prosecutor pointed at the prisoner.

'I can't be sure. It was a cold night, everyone was wrapped up well. He may or may not have been there.'

'Have you seen the prisoner before?'

'I have. I was returning from France late one night, with the lady and gentleman there,' Mr Lorry pointed at Doctor and Miss Manette.

'Miss Manette,' said the judge. 'Did you speak to the prisoner?'

All eyes in the courtroom turned to look at her.

'Yes, sir. He noticed that my father was very tired and asked if he could help. He was very kind. He told me he was travelling on business, with a false name. He had some papers with him and he was talking to some French gentlemen.'

There was more buzzing of blue flics.

'Doctor Manette,' continued the judge, 'do you remember this man?'

'I'm sorry, sir, I don't. I had just been released from a long time in prison and my mind was disturbed. Happily, I have recovered with the help of my loving daughter, but I remember nothing that happened that night.'

Another witness was then called. The defence lawyer asked if he was certain that the prisoner was the man on the mail coach. The man said he was quite sure and that he had never seen anyone like the prisoner before.

At this point, the defence lawyer asked another defence lawyer to stand up. 'This is my colleague, Mr Carton,' he said. 'Carton, would you please stand up?'

There was a cry from the court. Mr Carton and Charles Darnay were almost identical. The witness agreed that it could have been Mr Carton on the mail coach and not Mr Darnay.

By now Mr Cruncher's fingers were almost clean. It took another few minutes for the defence lawyer to paint the picture of John Barsad and Roger Cly as the true spies and Charles Darnay as an innocent man. The jury left to decide Darnay's fate, and ninety minutes later everything was over.

Mr Lorry handed a paper with one single word on it to Mr Cruncher. 'Quick! Take this message to the bank,' said Mr Lorry.

The word on the message was: *INNOCENT*, and Jerry Cruncher pushed his way through the buzzing crowds of confused and angry blue flies as they left the Old Bailey, perhaps in search of another prisoner to buzz around.

In the darkness of the court, only Doctor Manette, Miss Manette, Mr Lorry and Mr Carton were now left to say congratulations to Charles Darnay on his escape from the court, and from the grave.

Doctor Manette was now so very different from the shoemaker Mr

Lorry had saved from the room near the café in Paris. His daughter had brought him back from that terrible place: pulled him from his miserable past into the present.

The group broke up and soon only Darnay and Carton were left to make their way to a nearby hotel, in search of dinner.

'How do you feel to be free?' asked Sydney Carton.

'I'm not yet sure,' replied Darnay.

'You made quite an impression on Miss Manette,' continued Carton. His voice was bitter.

Darnay was surprised at Carton's comment. He was silent for a while, then tried to thank Carton for his help at the trial and, yet again, he was surprised when Carton answered, 'Do you think I particularly like you?'

'I hadn't asked myself this question,' replied Darnay, getting up to pay the bill, 'but I hope we can shake hands and that we can part without feeling bitter. Goodnight.'

Left alone, Sydney Carton stood up, walked over to a mirror and studied his face. He didn't like what he saw. 'Why should I like him,' he thought, 'just because he looks like me? No, he has just shown me what I could have been. I care about no-one on earth, and no-one on earth cares about me.'

The following morning, the sun rose sadly on the sight of Sydney Carton, a man of great abilities and good emotions who was unable to help himself. An unhappy man, who knew his faults, but did nothing about them, except let them eat away at him. ■

Stop & Check

1 Answer the questions about Chapter Three.

1 What differences are there between Jerry Cruncher and his son, young Jerry Cruncher?

____

2 Why do you think Jerry Cruncher was concerned about going into the court?

____

3 Why do you think people paid to go into courts at the time?

____

4 Describe the young man who was on trial.

____

5 Why do you think the people in the court are described as buzzing like flies?

____

6 Do you think that Barsad and Cly were honest?

____

7 Why do you think Darnay was found innocent?

____

8 Why was Doctor Manette so different now?

____

9 What impression did Darnay make on Miss Manette?

____

10 Why do you think Sydney Carton was so bitter?

____

2 What do I do? Write the Old Bailey jobs from Chapter Three next to the description.

1 It's my job to show that a person is guilty of a crime. I present proof and ask witnesses questions. ______________

2 It's my job to show that a person is innocent of a crime. I present proof and ask witnesses questions. ______________

3 I'm the president of the court. I make sure that everything is done legally and fairly. ______________

4 I open and close the door. I make sure that the right people come into the court. ______________

Grammar for First

3 Read the text below and think of the word which best fits each gap. Use only one word in each gap.

Tyburn

Tyburn was a terrible place (**1**)_________ London where criminals were hanged in (**2**)_________ past. It is very near to the area (**3**)_________ Marble Arch and the first hanging of a criminal there probably dates (**4**)_________ to the twelfth century. The early executions at Tyburn were almost (**5**)_________ public, as it wasn't until much later when executions were held in private. The place where people were hanged at Tyburn was, in later centuries, (**6**)_________ Tyburn Tree, and more than one person could be hanged at the same time. Public hangings were popular events; almost (**7**)_________ public holidays. The youngest person to (**8**)_________ executed at Tyburn was probably under the age of fourteen. The largest number of people who ever went to watch a public execution is thought to be about 200,000. The last person to face execution (**9**)_________ Tyburn was a man who had been found guilty of robbing people on a mail coach - just as the travellers feared (**10**)_________ Chapter One of *A Tale of Two Cities*.

Speaking

4 Crime and Punishment. Work in pairs to discuss these questions.

1 At the time Dickens was writing, capital punishment (execution) was common. Do you think this type of punishment is ever right?

2 What do you think should happen to someone who is found guilty of treason?

3 What punishment should be given to murderers?

4 What alternatives to prison should there be?

Writing & Speaking

5a **You are a court reporter. Make notes in the box below about what you saw during the trial of Charles Darnay.**

The atmosphere in the courtroom	The prisoner
What the prosecution said	Why the prisoner was found innocent

5b **Write an article for your newspaper about the trial of Charles Darnay. Write your article in the space below.**

5c **Work in pairs. Prepare a short TV news report about the trial and present your news item to another pair.**

Vocabulary

6a Adjectives and Prepositions. Complete these sentences with a preposition from the box.

on • of • in • by • at • of

1 People in the court were keen ______ watching criminal trials.
2 People were interested ______ Doctor and Miss Manette.
3 Darnay was suspected ______ being a traitor.
4 Darnay was found not guilty ______ treason.
5 The doorman was bored ______ the trial.
6 The defence lawyers were good ______ their jobs.

6b Write true sentences about yourself using these adjectives and prepositions. Remember that you need an *-ing* form if you follow a preposition with a verb.

- tired of ________________________________
- afraid of ________________________________
- keen on ________________________________

BEFORE-READING ACTIVITY

Speaking

7a In the next chapter, there is a terrible storm and Miss Manette imagines that she can hear footsteps of people who are about to come into their lives. Why do you think she feels like this? Discuss these possibilities:

a she plans to become involved in the French Revolution.
b she will become involved in the French Revolution, although she doesn't want to.
c people she loves will become involved in the French Revolution.

7b Talk about storms that you remember. Think about:

- where you were.
- what you saw.
- how you felt during the storm.

Chapter Four

The Marquis St. Evrémonde

▶ 5 Doctor and Miss Manette now lived in a quiet street in the centre of London and, about four months after the trial, Mr Jarvis Lorry was walking towards the house where he had been invited to lunch. Mr Lorry had become the doctor's friend and this quiet street was a sunny part of his life. Mr Lorry was a little early and the doctor and Miss Manette hadn't yet got home when he rang the doorbell. 'Is Miss Pross at home?' Mr Lorry asked the servant.

'Yes, sir,' was the reply, 'Please come in.'

Mr Lorry liked Miss Pross, the wild red-faced woman he had first met in Dover: he liked the way she cared for Lucie Manette. Today, however, she seemed a little upset. 'I don't like all these people who come here to see my little Lucie,' she stated.

'Are there very many?' asked Mr Lorry, a little surprised.

'Dozens,' she answered. 'No, *hundreds*!'

'Oh dear.'

'I have lived with my dear girl since she was ten years old and it's really very hard,' continued Miss Pross. 'Not one of them is good enough for her. Not one.'

'And how is the doctor?' Mr Lorry was keen to change the subject.

'Very well. But he never talks about his shoemaking time.'

Their conversation was interrupted when the doctor and his daughter came home. Lunchtime came and went, but *hundreds* of people did not. After dinner, as it was so warm, Lucie suggested they sit outside in the shade of a tree. There were still no *hundreds* of people, although Mr Darnay did arrive. They talked for a while about London and eventually Mr Darnay asked which of the old buildings they had visited.

'We went to the Tower of London, you know,' said Doctor Manette.

'Yes, I have been there, as I'm sure you all remember!' said Darnay. 'They told me a strange story about it, when I was there.'

'What was that?' asked Lucie.

'They were doing some building work, when they found an old cellar, deep under the ground. Every stone in the room was covered by names, dates and letters of prisoners' names. In the corner they found the letters D.I.G. and, of course, they realised that this was an instruction. They dug, and sure enough, in the corner, they found the remains of some paper and a bag. We'll never know what was on it, but the prisoner hid the paper from the prison guards.'

'Father! What's the matter?' cried Lucie.

Her father was standing up with his head in his hands, a look of horror on his face. 'Nothing, my dear, it's just started to rain.'

The small group made its way inside for tea. Tea time passed and there were still no *hundreds* of people. Mr Carton arrived a little later. The air outside was heavy as the rain turned into a storm. The group sat in the living room, listening to the sound of the rain and watching the lightning in the sky. They could hear the footsteps of people running to escape from the rain.

'It's like the echoes of the footsteps of people coming into our lives!' said Miss Manette, 'It feels like ...'

'If that's the case, there will be a great crowd of people coming into our lives soon!' said Sydney Carton, rudely interrupting her.

◈◈◈

In the other city in our story, one of the great lords of Paris, Monseigneur, one of many Monseigneurs, was holding his usual formal party. At that very moment, he was about to have his chocolate. Monseigneur had no difficulty swallowing[1] most things, and some would even say that he and his friends were swallowing France, but he still employed four servants and a cook to help him swallow the happy chocolate.

He had been out at supper the night before, a delightful little supper with the most charming company. Indeed he was out at the theatre or supper, or even both, most nights. He was a nobleman[2], a member of the government, with one particular idea of government: that everything should be allowed to go on in its own way, and that was particularly the case if good things came his way. Monseigneur's friends and family were of the same opinion; they were military officers with no military knowledge; officers in the navy who had never been on a ship; worldly priests with greedy eyes; governors who had no interest at all in government. They were all great gentlemen, from great families with no idea of real life. Their wives were the same: not one of them was happy to be called a mother. They brought their children into the world then quickly handed them over to poor women who raised them. As ever, dress was used to keep

1. swallowing: 吞嚥
2. nobleman: 貴族

all people in their places. Silk, gold and jewels, and everyone dressed for Life's Party.

Having swallowed his chocolate, Monseigneur was ready to welcome his guests. They bent their heads and waved their wrists, 'Your servant, sir.'

There was more bending and waving than you would expect in the kingdom of Heaven. Monseigneur passed through his rooms, promising things here and waving his hand there. At the final room, he turned round, walked back, promised and waved more, then was closed in once more by the chocolate fairies, to be seen no more.

His visitors left, leaving one man alone in the room, looking at the door of the chocolate room. 'Go to the Devil!' he said to the closed door and ran quietly downstairs. He was angry that the Monseigneur had not been warmer in his greeting. He got into his large carriage[1] and the driver drove off. His driver drove quickly just as his master, the Marquis St. Evrémonde, liked. The Marquis was still angry at the way he had been treated by Monseigneur, but he was enjoying the drive. He loved watching the ordinary people in the street running to get out of the way of his horses and carriage. The carriage raced through the streets and round corners, as women screamed and caught hold of their children. Finally, at a corner near a fountain, one of the wheels hit something and the carriage came to a stop. It was quite normal in these circumstances for the carriage to continue on its way immediately but, this time, twenty pairs of hands were holding on to the horses.

'What is it?' said the Marquis, calmly looking out of the carriage window. A tall man in nightclothes had picked something up from in front of the wheel and was crying loudly over it.

1. carriage: 舊時的四輪馬車

'I beg your pardon, Monsieur the Marquis,' said a man, 'it is a child.'

'Why is he making that terrible noise? Is it his child?'

'Excuse me, Monsieur the Marquis, but yes,' said the man.

The tall man suddenly got up from the ground and came running at the carriage. The Marquis reached for his sword.

'Killed! Dead!' shouted the tall man.

The people in the small square stared at the Marquis, who looked at them as if they were rats who had just come out of their holes. He took out his purse. 'You people can't even take care of your children!' he said. 'You might have injured the horses. Give the man that!' and he threw a gold coin into the crowd.

'Come Gaspard,' said another man who had just arrived on the scene. 'Be brave, your poor child died in a moment of play, in a moment without pain.'

'And who are you?' said the Marquis to the man.

'My name is Defarge.'

The Marquis threw another gold coin which landed at Defarge's feet. 'Take that,' he said, 'and spend it as you wish.'

Monsieur the Marquis leant back on his seat and calmly told his driver to set off. His comfort was disturbed when a gold coin flew into his carriage and rang on the floor. 'Hold the horses!' he said. 'Who threw that?'

He looked to the place where Defarge had been standing, but there was no-one there except a dark-haired woman, knitting.

'You dogs!' called the Marquis. 'I would happily ride over any of you with my horses!'

No-one dared look up at the carriage except the woman who was knitting. She looked up and stared directly into his face.

'Drive on,' commanded the Marquis.

He went off and more carriages soon drove by; the Minister, the Churchman, the Lawyer, the Doctor, and all the other guests at Life's Party. The rats stayed where they were, except the father, who had taken his dead child away. The dark-haired woman carried on knitting.

It was dark when Monsieur the Marquis's carriage, with its four horses, worked hard to climb the steep hill. He looked through the window at the village with its church, poor houses and castle, with the air of someone who was coming near home.

The village had one poor street with the usual poor small hotel, poor fountain and the usual crowds of poor people. It was clear why they were poor: taxes[1] for the state, taxes for the church, taxes for the Marquis and the local taxes. It was incredible that any of the village had been left for the future Marquis to swallow.

When they finally arrived at the castle with its rows of stone faces, servants opened the doors for him and the Marquis had one question, 'Has Monsieur Charles arrived from England yet?'

The answer was no.

In his rooms, the supper table was laid for two. After a quarter of an hour the Marquis was ready to eat. He sat down alone, but had only just swallowed his soup when there was the sound of wheels outside. It was his nephew and soon this nephew, known in England as Charles Darnay, was with his uncle.

They spoke about very little until coffee had been served and the servants had left.

1. taxes: 税

'I have come here for one reason,' said Charles to the Marquis.

'Do tell me why,' the Marquis said, in an elegant tone.

'We have done wrong and the people hate us,' Charles answered. 'The Evrémonde name is hated everywhere.'

'*We* have done wrong? Surely not,' replied the Marquis, coldly. 'I shall *die* to protect all that we have created. *You*, I see, are lost.'

'I no longer want to be a French citizen: I want to give up my claim to this castle, and settle in England,' said Charles.

'When I die, this castle and land will belong to you. You can't change that and neither can I.'

The Marquis stopped, observed his nephew and added, 'And, do you know another Frenchman in England, a doctor, with a daughter?'

'Yes, I do,' said Charles, a little surprised.

'I thought so,' said the Marquis, with a slight cruel smile. 'Goodnight. We will speak again in the morning.'

The taxed and the taxers in the village were asleep. Dogs barked in the distance. Then the sun began its long journey up, turning the water in the fountain blood red, like the wine from the broken barrel. Now the sun was full up and the windows in the village opened. Men and women set off to work, while the castle was still asleep. There was one stone face too many there this morning: it lay on the Marquis St. Evrémonde's pillow. His face was a fine mask. A knife had been pushed through a piece of paper and then through his heart. The message on the paper read:

Drive him fast to his grave, Jacques.

Stop & Check

1 Correct the false information in this summary of Chapter Four. There are seven factual errors.

Miss Manette and her father are now living in a quiet street in the centre of Paris. Mr Lorry, Sydney Carton and Jerry Cruncher sometimes visit them. One day, Doctor Manette gets very upset when he hears about something hidden by a prisoner in the Tower of London.

In Paris, the Marquis St. Evrémonde's carriage kills three children by driving too fast. When he returns to his castle, we find out that he is waiting for his son, Charles Darnay, to arrive from England. Charles tells him that he no longer wants to live in France and that he has decided to move to Italy. The Marquis asks whether Charles knows Mr Lorry and his daughter. That night, the Marquis St. Evrémonde is shot while he's sleeping.

Vocabulary

2 Rich and Poor. Fill the gaps in the text below with words from the box.

wealthy • poor • taxes • servants • poverty • noblemen

Dickens believed that the French Revolution was caused by the **(1)**________ aristocrats and governors of France. He believed that the revolution became inevitable, as the (**2**)________ of the majority of the population was ignored. The behaviour of the local (**3**)________, or Monseigneurs, is contrasted with the lives of the (**4**)________. The Marquis St. Evrémonde is an arrogant example of a Monseigneur: he treats his (**5**)________ badly. The villagers who live on his land have to pay (**6**)________ to him, even though they are poor and hungry.

Speaking & Writing

3a Do you agree with the following quotations and sayings? Discuss your answers in pairs.

1 Money makes the world go round. *From the musical, Cabaret*
2 Money can't buy you happiness, but it sure helps! *Anon*
3 The love of money is the root of all evil. *The Bible*
4 Money speaks sense in a language all nations can understand. *Aphra Behn*
5 A fool and his money are soon parted. *Dr John Bridges*
6 Time is money. *Benjamin Franklin*

3b Write a paragraph about how important money is in your life.

Vocabulary

4a Match the phrasal verbs with *off* to their meanings.

1 ☐	turn off	a	go bad
2 ☐	take off	b	stop something from working
3 ☐	set off	c	stop having an effect
4 ☐	keep off	d	start
5 ☐	go off	e	not go somewhere
6 ☐	wear off	f	remove

4b Now put the correct phrasal verb into the context sentence. Be careful with the verb form.

1 We _________ late, so we missed the plane.
2 You should always _________ the TV when you leave a room.
3 _________ the grass!
4 The aspirin's _________. I think I'll take another.
5 It smells terrible, I think the milk has _________.
6 _________ your coat! It's hot in here.

Grammar for First

5 **Use the word given in capitals at the end of some of the lines to form a word that fits in the gap in the same line.**

Chocolate

Chocolate is (**1**)_________ from cacao beans	**MAKE**
(also called cocoa beans) and most cacao	
is grown in Africa, although the cacao tree	
(**2**)_________ originated in the Americas.	**ACTUAL**
The Aztecs and Mayans both used cacao in	
bitter drinks, (**3**)_________the Europeans,	**LIKE**
who added sugar and milk to (**4**)_________	**SWEET**
it, when chocolate was introduced in the	
sixteenth century. Chocolate is thought to	
have a (**5**)_________ effect on serotonin levels	**POWER**
in the brain and (**6**)_________ are currently	**RESEARCH**
working to (**7**)_________ other positive and	**IDENTIFICATION**
negative effects. It is poisonous to some	
animals, (**8**)_________ mice, rats, cats and	**INCLUDE**
dogs. Chocolate is (**9**)_________ added to	**COMMON**
cakes and biscuits in many parts of the world	
and in Europe and the United States, excessive	
(**10**)_________ may have increased obesity rates.	**CONSUME**

Writing

6 **Summary Writing. Write a short summary of the Marquis's journey from Paris to his castle. Include the connectors below in your summary.**

although • in spite of • however

Word-building

7a Prefixes. Use prefixes from the box to build the opposites of these adjectives. Check your answers in a dictionary.

un-	im-	in-	il-	ir-

1 _un_ comfortable
2 ___ relevant
3 ___ logical
4 ___ fortunate
5 ___ edible
6 ___ regular
7 ___ literate
8 ___ conscious
9 ___ patient

7b Rewrite these sentences using one of the adjectives from 7a.

1 The prisoner was not a lucky man. The prisoner was ________.
2 Many of the poor couldn't read or write. They were ________.
3 The Marquis couldn't wait to get home. He was ___________.

BEFORE-READING ACTIVITY

Listening

▶ 6 **8 Read the questions below and use your knowledge of the text to guess the answers. Now listen and check.**

1 What is Darnay now doing?
  a ☐ Teaching French in England.
  b ☐ Teaching English in France.
  c ☐ Looking for a job with the government.
2 How does Darnay feel about Lucie Manette?
  a ☐ He likes her, but is in love with someone else.
  b ☐ He likes her, but hopes she will marry Sydney Carton.
  c ☐ He loves her, and wants to marry her.
3 Someone else has recently visited Lucie. Who is it?
  a ☐ Mr Lorry.
  b ☐ Sydney Carton.
  c ☐ John Barsad, the spy.
4 Why doesn't Darnay tell Doctor Manette his real name?
  a ☐ Doctor Manette doesn't want to know his real name.
  b ☐ Darnay doesn't want anyone to know his real name.
  c ☐ Darnay is afraid that Sydney Carton will steal his identity.

Chapter Five

The Register

▶ 6 Twelve months later, Mr Charles Darnay was teaching French to young men in England. He had done well and had worked hard. He was, of course, in love with Lucie Manette. He had not yet spoken to her about his real family name of Evrémonde, or his uncle's death, and he had not yet spoken to Lucie, or her father, about his love.

One summer's day, he visited Doctor Manette. 'I must speak to you, sir, about Lucie.'

'Oh,' said the doctor, looking down at the floor.

'I love her. She doesn't know this, yet. I haven't told her and I've never written to her, but I love her.'

'I have no doubt of this.'

'I don't know whether she loves me. I know she loves you, her dearest father and that she loves the memory of her mother, your dear love.'

'Don't talk about that,' said the old man, upset. 'I will speak to Lucie.'

'Thank you, sir. But there is one thing I must tell you. You know that Darnay is not my real name. I want to tell you what my real name is and explain why I am in England.'

'Stop!' Doctor Manette put his hands over his ears. 'You can tell me if Lucie agrees to marry you, tell me on your wedding day, but do not tell me now!'

When Lucie came home a little later, her father was not sitting in his usual reading chair. Upstairs, she could hear a tap-tap-tap sound coming from his bedroom. She ran lightly upstairs and opened the door, and her blood ran cold as she saw her father's head, bent low, as he formed leather into the shape of a shoe. He thought he was back in prison!

Charles Darnay was not the only person in love with Lucie Manette. Soon after Charles had spoken to her father, Lucie herself had a caller, Sydney Carton. He had often been a little rude when he visited the Manette house and today was no different. He started by telling her how terrible his life was, how lazy he was, how he wasted his time on pleasure.

'Why not change your life?' was Lucie's gentle reply.

'It's too late,' replied Sydney, sadly. 'Unless you will love me, save me from myself, I can only sink lower! And you can't love me: it's hopeless, I know.'

Lucie was very kind, but Sydney left knowing that she could never love him and having promised one very fine thing: that he would do anything in his power to help her or, as he said, *'a life you love'* at any time in the future.

◈◈◈

Mr Jerry Cruncher sat in his usual chair outside Tellson's Bank, thinking contentedly about his life and work, and unhappily about his wife's continual praying. Suddenly, he heard shouts from further down the street. 'Spy! Spy!' he heard. It then became clear that there was a funeral and that the man in question had been an Old Bailey spy. None other, in fact, than Roger Cly who had given evidence against Charles Darnay. Mr Cruncher left his chair to his son and followed the body to its grave at the cemetery. As the crowd grew, it got louder and louder and more and more dangerous, until it was an uncontrollable mob[1]. Shopkeepers closed up and windows were broken. Cries of 'Spy! Spy!' echoed from people who had never been near the Old Bailey in their lives. Then a rumour that soldiers were coming caused the mob to start melting away.

Jerry Cruncher made his way home and, as usual, shouted at his wife for 'praying against him' and announced his intention to go fishing that night. Young Jerry was sent to bed early and then, at one o'clock in the morning, Mr Cruncher got up from his chair, picked up a large bag, some chains and a rope, and left the house. He didn't realise that his son had been pretending to be asleep and was a minute or two behind him as he walked through London, determined to find out where his father went fishing at night and how his fingers got so dirty.

Along the way, Mr Cruncher met another fisherman friend and then a little further along, another. By the light of the watery moon, young Jerry watched the three men as they climbed over the iron gate into the cemetery. They didn't go far before they started to '*fish*'.

They used tools at first, then they started to pull something up from the grave. A body! Young Jerry ran.

The following morning, as they walked to Tellson's Bank, young Jerry asked his father a very difficult question. 'Why do people take bodies from cemeteries?'

1. mob: 暴民

'Hmm. I think they sell them to doctors,' Mr Cruncher said, nervously.

'I think I'd like to do that when I grow up,' said his son in a serious voice.

Jerry couldn't have been more shocked.

◈◈◈

There were more people in the Defarge café than usual this morning. There had been more than usual on Monday and Tuesday, too. Monsieur Defarge, Jacques One, Jacques Two and Jacques Three were listening to a story being told by a mender of roads from the country. 'Gaspard was a good man, but they say he was driven mad when his child was killed by the Marquis,' said the mender of roads.

'And by the fact that the Marquis didn't care,' said Defarge.

'Yes, so I believe. Gaspard killed the Marquis the same night and then he hid with good friends near where I live. He was safe for almost a year. Then, they came,' continued the mender of roads.

'Who came?' asked Jacques Three.

'Six soldiers. They came one morning and they took him to prison. He was executed, then they left his body hanging high above the fountain in the village.'

'No!' cried Jacques Two.

'Yes. It poisoned the water and its shadow poisoned the air of the village.'

'What do you think Jacques?' said Jacques One, when the mender of roads had moved away, in search of something to eat.

'To be registered[1]. I'm sure. Registered for death. The whole

1. registered: 記錄

Evrémonde family must be put on the register.'

'Are you sure that the register is safe?'

'Oh yes,' said Defarge, 'my wife knits the register. Only she can read it, no-one else. It's perfectly safe.'

'And will this mender of roads talk about us?' Jacques Three was worried.

'No,' went on Defarge. 'He's a simple man. Do you know something? He wants to see the King and Queen, before he goes back to his village!'

Sunday came and Monsieur and Madame Defarge took the mender of roads to the royal palace at Versailles. Madame knitted all the way there and all the way back. He was so impressed by the gold, silver and beautiful jewels of the royal family and of all the ladies and gentlemen, that the mender of roads took off his blue cap and shouted, 'Long Live the King, Long Live the Queen, Long Live everyone and everything!'

The mender of roads was then worried about his enthusiasm, but Monsieur Defarge wasn't worried, 'You made them all believe that the people love them. They think they will last forever, so they will get worse and worse, and change will come sooner.'

Madame Defarge continued knitting.

Monsieur and Madame Defarge went back to the warmth of their café, while the mender of roads started his long journey back to his home village, thinking about the things he had seen on his way to Paris. The customers in the café were talking excitedly. 'Doctor Manette lived with you here, didn't he? I mean, after he was freed from the Bastille,' said one man.

'Yes,' agreed Monsieur Defarge.

'His daughter came here to find him, didn't she,' he asked again.

'She did. We had a letter to say they were safely in England, but that was five years or so ago.'

'It's a small world, isn't it? Miss Manette is going to marry the nephew of the man Gaspard killed!'

Monsieur Defarge looked shocked, but Madame continued knitting.

'His name', said the man, 'is Charles Darnay. He uses his mother's name, but now his uncle is dead, he is the new Marquis St. Evrémonde.'

Madame Defarge added a new name to her knitted register, while her husband commented that it would be better if Charles Darnay never returned to France.

◇◇◇

On the night before Lucie's wedding to Charles, she and Doctor Manette sat outside enjoying the warm evening air. 'Look at the moon,' he said. 'I often looked at it from my prison and wondered about the child I didn't know. It has been my greatest joy to spend these years with you and to know that the shadows of my life have not affected yours.'

The following morning, Darnay went to speak to his future father-in-law. Mr Lorry and Miss Pross were very concerned to make sure that Lucie wasn't worried about her father. 'All the time you are away on your honeymoon, Lucie, your father will be in very good hands,' declared Mr Lorry.

When Charles and Doctor Manette left his study, the doctor was very pale. Mr Lorry was the only one to notice how different he looked; as if a cold wind had cut him to the bone.

They went quickly to the church and after a short, but happy service, Charles and Lucie were married. They left immediately for a two-week honeymoon.

Mr Lorry and Miss Pross were now both very concerned about the doctor. As soon as they took him home, he started making shoes again. Mr Lorry had to go to Tellson's Bank, but promised to come back later in the evening to check on Doctor Manette.

On his return, Miss Pross met him at the door. 'Oh, Mr Lorry, come and look. The doctor doesn't know me. He doesn't know who I am!'

'What are you making, old friend?' asked Mr Lorry, walking into the doctor's room.'

'A young lady's walking shoe. Now leave me alone. I must finish it soon.'

Mr Lorry and Miss Pross made sure that the doctor was never left alone. On the ninth day, Mr Lorry fell asleep while he was watching Doctor Manette. When he woke up, there was the doctor, sitting in his reading chair. His face was pale, but he was reading carefully. He seemed to have no memory of the last nine days and was, in fact, convinced that his daughter had been married the day before.

Mr Lorry and Miss Pross carefully told the doctor everything. He listened carefully and he also listened to Mr Lorry's suggestion that his shoemaking tools and bench should be taken away. 'I don't think you should keep them,' said Mr Lorry, firmly.

The old man was unsure, but finally agreed. The bench was to be burned and the tools were to be taken away and buried.

Stop & Check

1 Put these nine events into the order they appear in Chapter Five.

1 ☐ Doctor Manette falls ill again.

2 ☐ Jerry Cruncher goes to a funeral.

3 ☐ Lucie and Charles go on their honeymoon.

4 ☐ Charles Darnay tells Doctor Manette that he wants to marry Lucie.

5 ☐ Lucie and Charles get married.

6 ☐ Sydney Carton tells Lucie that he's in love with her.

7 ☐ The mender of roads tells everyone in the café about Gaspard's death.

8 ☐ We find out why Madame Defarge knits so much.

9 ☐ Jerry Cruncher's son sees his father digging up a body.

Vocabulary

2 Look again at page 57 of Chapter Five. Find words that mean the same as the words below. The words are in the same order in the text.

1 marriage ____________

2 noise ____________

3 jail ____________

4 impolite ____________

5 fun ____________

6 unhappily ____________

7 useless ____________

8 good ____________

9 happily ____________

Writing

3 Young Jerry Cruncher has a frightening experience. Write about a time when you have felt frightened. Organize your writing into paragraphs and use a few of the following sequencers.

first of all • at first • after that • then • after a short time
not long after • quite soon after • finally

Speaking

4a Read the different opinions about the characters in *A Tale of Two Cities*. Which do you agree with?

		agree	disagree
1	'Despite his *fishing*, Jerry Cruncher is really a likeable character.'	☐	☐
2	'Sydney Carton should stop complaining and change his life.'	☐	☐
3	'Doctor Manette's mind is still very fragile.'	☐	☐
4	'Lucie is a very unkind woman.'	☐	☐
5	'Madame Defarge is less committed to the revolution than her husband.'	☐	☐
6	'Monsieur Defarge is a cruel man.'	☐	☐
7	'Charles Darnay is wrong to marry Lucie.'	☐	☐

4b Work in pairs to discuss your answers. Give reasons for your opinions.

5 Read the information about Paris. Decide which answer – A, B, C or D best fits each gap.

Paris

Paris has always been (**1**)________ one of the most romantic capital cities in the world. Situated on the river Seine, it has been inhabited since at (**2**)________ the third century B.C.. The Romans were the first to build defensive structures in the city. Paris (**3**)________ a capital city in 987 and continued to expand in later centuries. The most important political events seen by Paris (**4**)________ the 1789 Revolution and the Paris Peace Conference at the end of the First World War. Visitors to Paris today can see world-famous (**5**)________, such as the Eiffel Tower, the Arc de Triomphe, the Cathedral of Notre-Dame de Paris and the more modern Pompidou Centre. They can also see wonderful art at many museums, the most famous of which is probably the Louvre. Other tourist attractions include numerous parks and gardens, the (**6**)________ Palace of Versailles, the city's street markets and even its cemeteries.

Paris is also considered one of the capitals of world cooking and visitors can enjoy a (**7**)________ variety of restaurants, bistros, and cafés.

Travelling around is easy, with Paris's excellent (**8**)________ of underground trains and buses.

	A	B	C	D
1	☐ considered	☐ known	☐ viewed	☐ seen
2	☐ first	☐ start	☐ least	☐ last
3	☐ began	☐ became	☐ made	☐ done
4	☐ include	☐ including	☐ added	☐ numbering
5	☐ landmarks	☐ visions	☐ squares	☐ sites
6	☐ nearby	☐ near	☐ by	☐ close
7	☐ deep	☐ enormous	☐ broad	☐ wide
8	☐ mixture	☐ set	☐ network	☐ route

Speaking

6 Giving Opinions. Discuss the questions below in pairs, using phrases from the box.

Personally, I think that ... It's a difficult question, but I feel that ... I know that ..., but ... I'm not sure, but ... I'm absolutely certain that ...

- Would you like to emigrate like Charles and Lucie? Why/Why not?
- Which country would you most like to live in for a long period of time? Why?
- Do you think it's better to live in the same place all your life, or to move about?
- What do you think migrants miss about their home countries?
- What are the reasons why people might emigrate?

BEFORE-READING ACTIVITY

Listening

7a Read the true/false questions below and use your knowledge of the text to guess the answers.

		T	F
1	Sydney Carton talks to Charles after he and Lucie come back from their honeymoon.	☐	☐
2	Sydney Carton wants Charles and himself to be friends.	☐	☐
3	Charles says something unkind about Carton.	☐	☐
4	Lucie thinks that Carton is much nicer than he seems.	☐	☐
5	Charles doesn't like Carton at all.	☐	☐
6	Charles promises always to remember something that Lucie has said.	☐	☐

▶ 7 **7b Listen to the first part of Chapter Five and check your answers.**

Chapter Six

East, West, South and North

▶ 7 When Charles and Lucie Darnay came back to London from their honeymoon, Sydney Carton was their first visitor. Carton spoke to Charles, asking him to forgive him for being rude after the trial and offering him the hand of friendship. Charles assured Sydney that he had forgotten all about it, but at dinner, after Sydney had gone home, Charles made some general comments about his lack of responsibility. His wife was silent at dinner, but after Doctor Manette and Miss Pross had gone to bed, she sat staring thoughtfully into the fire.

'What is it, my dear?' asked Charles.

'I don't think you were very kind to Mr Carton this afternoon. I know he seems like a rude, lazy man, but there is more to his character than this.'

'I don't think too badly of him, really.' Her husband was surprised.

'I know, but Mr Carton has a heart, which he shows very rarely. His heart is broken, I have seen it bleed.'

'I'll remember this as long as I live,' Charles replied, touched by how much his wife cared.

◈◈◈

The years passed and Lucie had a daughter now, also called Lucie, who was six years old. Charles Darnay was a strong, wealthy man and both her father and Miss Pross were well and happy. Sydney Carton visited them a few times a year and Lucie listened to the footsteps of the years. There had been sadness as well as joy: their young, golden-haired, son had died. Now there was just little Lucie to chat away in the tongues of the Two Cities that were important in their lives.

At the same time, there were other echoes from a distance, too. There was the sound of thunder from the other City, the sound of the great storm in France and the dreadful sea that was rising on that July evening in 1789 ...

... Mad dangerous footsteps were forcing their way through the streets of Saint Antoine, footsteps not easily made clean again once they were stained red. A huge shout had come from the throat of Saint Antoine that morning, and at the centre of that angry screaming mob was Defarge's café. Young and old took hold of knives, guns and swords, tools they found on their farms and in their workshops. Others armed themselves with rocks and stones.

'Jacques One, Jacques Two, Jacques Three stay near me!' shouted Defarge.

Madame Defarge was not knitting today. She stood calmly near her husband, in her right hand was a long knife, and in her belt were a small gun and another, shorter, knife.

'Come then!' cried Defarge. 'Patriots and friends we are ready! To the Bastille!'

With a shout that sounded as if all the breath in France had been shaped into that one hated word *Bastille*, the living sea rose, wave after wave and flowed to that very place. Alarm bells rang, drums sounded. The eight great towers of the Bastille stayed strong for four hours against the waves of angry people. Then a white handkerchief appeared. The Bastille had fallen! The sea of people became an ocean and flooded in through the great gates.

'The prisoners!'

'The records!'

'The secret cells[1]!'

'The prisoners!'

At one point, Defarge caught hold of a prison officer. 'What is the meaning of One Hundred and Five North Tower?' he screamed at the terrified man.

'Monsieur, it's a cell. I'll take you there!'

They pushed though the mob of people and found the cell. It was a small room with a window high in one of the walls. There was a chair, a table and a small bed. On the wall, were two letters.

'A. M.!' cried Defarge. 'Alexandre Manette!'

He began to search the room. He broke the table, the chair and the bed. Then, in the wall, he saw something white. A document! Defarge took the document, set fire to the furniture and the men left the cell.

The sea of people of Saint Antoine was anxious to have Defarge at their head: they had found the Governor of the Bastille and wanted to make sure he couldn't escape: they were taking him to the court at the Hôtel de Ville for trial. Madame Defarge stood near to the Governor as the mob began to attack him. She didn't try to save him, and when he was dead, it was she who took out her long knife and cut off his head on the steps of the Hôtel de Ville.

The sea of black and threatening waters rolled on. Carried with

1. cells: 單間牢房

them were two sets of seven faces, different from all the rest. They were seven prisoners released from their cells by the storm and carried high on the shoulders of the mob. The other seven faces were carried higher still; seven dead faces of guards killed by the mob.

Through the streets of Paris, the footsteps of Saint Antoine echoed in the middle of July, in the year 1789. The footsteps were mad and dangerous and the stains they made would not be as easily cleaned as they were when they were stained red by the broken barrel of wine.

Saint Antoine had one delighted week of brotherly affection and congratulations. Madame Defarge looked around her café and at the street outside. They were no longer afraid of spies, as the spies were less keen to come into the neighbourhood. She could see the poor and the unemployed: they now had a job to do. Madame Defarge had a look of approval on her face. She could see the knitting women with their cruel fingers and she was the leader of this group.

A companion sitting next to her was knitting red caps for the people. People called this short, rather fat, grocer's wife *The Vengeance*[1]. 'Listen!' shouted The Vengeance. 'Someone's coming.'

'It's Defarge!'

Defarge ran into the café. 'I have news from the other world!' he cried, pulling off his red cap. 'Do you remember Foulon, who told the hungry that they could eat grass?'

'We do!' came the cry from all throats. 'And now he's dead!'

'No, he *isn't* dead! He was so afraid of us that he pretended to be dead: he even had a funeral. He's alive and was hiding in the country. He's now a prisoner and they're taking him to the Hôtel de Ville!'

There was a moment of silence.

1. The Vengeance: 復仇者

'Patriots!' said Defarge in a determined voice. 'Are we ready?'

A second later, Madame Defarge's knife and gun were in her belt, drums could be heard in the streets and The Vengeance was knocking on doors, screaming at the women to follow her. 'Foulon! Foulon! We have Foulon! The man who told us our hungry babies could eat grass!'

Armed men and women flowed out of Saint Antoine so fast, that in a quarter of an hour, only a few tiny children and the elderly who couldn't run, were left there.

Foulon, the old, ugly man, was in the Examination Hall at the Hôtel de Ville, when Madame Defarge, her husband, The Vengeance and Jacques Three ran in.

'Look!' cried Madame Defarge. 'He's in ropes. Let's take him outside and make him eat grass!'

'Bring him out! Bring him out!' cried the mob in the street.

The old man was taken outside and hundreds of hands pushed grass into his face, as he was taken away to his death. Madame Defarge let him go, like a cat might have done to a mouse.

This was not the end of this bad day's work. Saint Antoine's blood was boiling as it heard that Foulon's son-in-law was coming into Paris with five hundred soldiers. Five hundred soldiers were not enough to stop the mob from killing him too.

It was late at night when the men and women came back to their crying, hungry children. Long lines of them queued up at the miserable bakers' shops to buy bad bread to fill their empty stomachs. They talked quietly about the day's successes then, and again at home, as they ate their poor suppers.

It was almost morning when the last of the customers left Defarge's café.

'The time has come,' said Defarge to his wife.

'Almost,' was her reply.

Saint Antoine slept, the Defarges slept: even The Vengeance slept with her hungry family. The drum was at rest.

There was a change in the village with the fountain. The prison on the hill didn't seem as threatening as it had once seemed. There were fewer soldiers to guard it. The fields around were still as dry and poor as the miserable people. Everything was still broken. Houses, fences, animals, men, women and children were all still worn out.

The Monseigneur was often a fine gentleman; offering a polite example of a shining life. But wasn't it strange that the Monseigneurs had somehow caused all this to happen? Everyone else had nothing. The Monseigneurs were beginning to run away from things, now they had swallowed the last drop of blood from the people.

Things began to change with the appearance of strange, unfamiliar faces to replace the fine features of Monseigneur. Such a man came to the village, like a ghost, at midday in the July weather. He saw the mender of roads at his work, in his new red cap. 'How are things going, Jacques?' he said.

'All well, Jacques,' said the mender of roads. 'No food, but all's well.'

'There's no food anywhere,' said Jacques. 'It's tonight.'

'Tonight?' said the mender of roads. 'Where?'

'Here. Where's the castle?'

The mender of roads gave the stranger directions and went back to work.

There was a whisper in the village and after their poor supper, the villagers didn't go back to bed. They stood, near the fountain, waiting for something to happen. The villagers were all looking in the same direction and Monsieur Gabelle, the head tax collector of the place, was worried. He went up to the top of his house and looked in the same direction as the villagers.

The night got deeper. Four figures, East, West, South and North walked through the woods and into the castle. Four lights started to shine in four different places, but soon the castle began to be visible by some strange light of its own. The doors and windows were lit as the light grew higher, wider and brighter.

The few servants who were left there ran or rode away as the fire got stronger. They ran, or rode, to the village to ask for Monsieur Gabelle's help, but he could do nothing. The mender of roads and two hundred and fifty of his friends, all called Jacques, were standing by the fountain, all wearing their red caps. 'The castle must burn,' they said with one voice.

Monsieur Gabelle was lucky; he escaped with his life. There were other tax collectors in other villages across France who were less lucky that night. East, West, South and North travelled through the country and the fires burned.

Reading for First

1 Look again at pages 68 and 69. Choose the answer – A, B, C or D which you think fits best according to the text.

1 Why was Lucie so silent at dinner after Charles had spoken about Sydney?

A ☐ She was very angry.
B ☐ She was thinking about something.
C ☐ She disliked talking about other people.
D ☐ She thought her husband was irresponsible.

2 What did Dickens mean by 'Lucie listened to the footsteps of the years'?

A ☐ Lucie was very imaginative.
B ☐ Her father often walked around during the day.
C ☐ Lucie was getting older and the echo of footsteps is a theme in the book.
D ☐ Lucie was worrying about the future.

3 How did Dickens describe the beginning of the revolution in France?

A ☐ Like a great storm and a terrible ocean rising.
B ☐ Like an echo in the distance.
C ☐ Like a normal July evening.
D ☐ Like any other historical event.

4 Why wouldn't the footsteps be easy to clean this time?

A ☐ This time, there were too many footsteps.
B ☐ People were too busy with the revolution.
C ☐ The marks would last because they were blood, not wine.
D ☐ People were too angry to clean them.

5 Why wasn't Madame Defarge knitting today?

A ☐ There were too many people in Defarge's café.
B ☐ Her husband was making a speech to the patriots.
C ☐ She had never been to the Bastille before.
D ☐ She was preparing to fight with the other patriots.

Word-building

2a Complete the word-building table. You can use your dictionary.

Noun	Verb	Adjective(s)
dread		
	care	
	strengthen	
	sleep	
	widen	
blood		
misery	----	

2b Choose adjectives from the table to complete these sentences. More than one answer may be possible.

1 It was late and the villagers were all ____________.
2 They left ____________ footsteps all through Saint Antoine.
3 The gates of the Bastille were very ____________.
4 Charles thought Lucie was a very ____________ woman.
5 There were long queues in the ____________ bakers' shops.
6 Dickens compares the beginning of the revolution to 'a ____________ sea'.

Grammar

3 Active and Passive. Complete this extract from a newspaper article about the taking of the Bastille using the verbs in brackets. Look out for passives and check your tenses.

Today, in France there (**1**)_____ (be) confusion about the situation at the terrible prison called the Bastille. Patriots attacked the towers and the gates (**2**)_____ (break down) after about four hours' fighting. A white handkerchief (**3**)_____ (wave) from one of the towers and the patriots knew they (**4**)_____ (win).

The prisoners in the Bastille (**5**)_____ (release) and the Governor of the Bastille (**6**)_____ (take) to the Hôtel de Ville, where he (**7**)_____ (execute) by the mob. Seven guards from the prison (**8**)_____ (kill) and seven prisoners (**9**)_____ (carry) through the streets of Paris. No-one knows where this (**10**)_____ (end).

Characters

4a Which of the adjectives in the box would you use to describe the following characters in *A Tale of Two Cities?*

dangerous • brave • loyal • vengeful • bloodthirsty angry • miserable • rude • happy • responsible

1 Miss Manette ____________

2 Charles Darnay ____________

3 Sydney Carton ____________

4 Madame Defarge ____________

5 Monsieur Defarge ____________

6 The patriots ____________

7 The poor ____________

4b Compare your answer with a partner's.

Speaking

5 Work in pairs, following the instructions below.

Student A, look at the pictures on Page 35 and Page 97. Compare the two pictures and say how you think the men are feeling in the two different pictures.

Student B, listen to your partner and count the number of adjectives s/he uses!

Now, **Student B**, look at the pictures on Page 71 and Page 111. Compare the two pictures and say why you think the people are all in the street.

Student A, it's your turn to count the number of adjectives your partner uses!

Vocabulary

6 Which of these words is the odd one out? Write your reasons below.

1 ☐ rock ☐ stone ☐ earth ☐ grass

2 ☐ knife ☐ gun ☐ belt ☐ sword

3 ☐ anxious ☐ threatening ☐ worried ☐ concerned

4 ☐ rope ☐ wood ☐ chain ☐ string

5 ☐ fountain ☐ ocean ☐ river ☐ sea

BEFORE-READING ACTIVITY

Writing

7a The next chapter sees a major change in the Darnay family's life. The first line is in the box below. Continue the story from your own imagination.

Little Lucie had celebrated three more birthdays when the footsteps from France echoed once more in the Darnay's family life.

7b Now read Chapter Seven and compare the events with your own story.

Chapter Seven

A Message from Gabelle

▶ 8 Little Lucie had celebrated three more birthdays when the footsteps from France echoed once more in the Darnay home.

By August of the year 1792, royalty no longer existed in France and Monseigneur, when he had been able, had left France. Tellson's Bank was the meeting place of the Monseigneurs who had made their way to London. They now had no money, so they gathered in a place where their money used to be.

One day, Mr Lorry was sitting at his desk at Tellson's and Charles Darnay was standing near it, talking to him. 'Mr Lorry, you mustn't go!'

'Am I too old?'

'The weather, a difficult journey, a changing country, Paris that may not even be safe for you. It's not a question of age!'

'But I can be of some help to Tellson's in Paris.'

'I wish I were going myself,' said Darnay.

'Don't be ridiculous,' came the reply. 'Stay here and look after your Lucies. I'll take Jerry Cruncher with me when I go tonight.'

The two men were interrupted when someone put a letter onto Mr Lorry's desk. The address, when translated into English, read:

Urgent. To Monsieur, the Marquis St. Evrémonde, of France. Care of Tellson & Co., Bankers, London, England.

On his wedding day, Darnay had told Doctor Manette about his true identity, but the doctor had made him promise never to tell anyone that he was from the Evrémonde family. No-one but the doctor knew his real name.

'No-one knows where this gentleman is,' said Mr Lorry.

It was true. Mr Lorry had shown the letter to this Monseigneur and that Monseigneur and nobody had a good word to say about the Marquis and nobody knew where he was. Now, in Mr Lorry's office, everyone was keen to insult the new Monseigneur.

'I know the man,' said Darnay. 'I'll take the letter to him.'

'Thank you,' said Mr Lorry, simply.

'What time are you and Jerry leaving for Paris?'

On hearing the answer eight o'clock, Darnay promised to be there to say goodbye to Mr Lorry and left, with the letter. As soon as he was outside, he read the contents:

Prison of the Abbaye, Paris.

June 21, 1792.

Monsieur,

My life has been in danger for many months and now I have been brought here, to Paris. My house has been destroyed – burned to the ground.

My trial is soon to start and the trial is for treason. I need your help: I have committed no crime, but I have acted as your tax collector. Why are you not here to speak for me? I, who have always done my duty to you and your family. For the love of Heaven and Justice, for the honour of your family name, I beg you to come to Paris and speak for me!

Your servant,

Gabelle.

An old servant, and a good man! How could Darnay refuse to help him? Darnay knew very well that his uncle had treated the villagers badly and had been responsible for many evil things. Darnay also knew that he himself had failed Gabelle and the other servants, by staying here in London, in his happy family home with Lucie, and not using his influence to help in the country of his birth.

Charles Darnay had already started to make his decision. In his mind, he had no choice; he had to go to Paris. He was being pulled back into the Evrémonde family and the country he had abandoned long ago.

Charles walked through the streets around Tellson's Bank, thinking about his plan. Lucie must not know until he had gone and neither must Doctor Manette. He decided not to tell Mr Lorry, although he would make himself known as soon as they were both in Paris. It was now time for him to return to Tellson's and wave goodbye to Mr Lorry.

The coach and horses were outside the bank and Jerry Cruncher was ready to go.

'I took your letter to the Marquis,' said Charles. 'He told me his answer.'

'Fine,' said Mr Lorry, taking out his notebook.

'There is a prisoner at the Abbaye.'

'His name?'

'Gabelle. The message is simple. The man has received the message and will come,' said Charles. 'He will start on his journey tomorrow night.'

That night, it was the fourteenth of August, Charles Darnay

stayed up late. He wrote two letters, one to Lucie and the other to the Doctor. The next day was hard, but when it came to evening, Charles made an excuse and left the house. The unseen force was pulling him to France. Gabelle's request was in his sinking heart as he left everything that was dear to him and sailed towards Paris.

The journey to Paris was slow. Every town and every village had a group of citizen patriots who stopped everyone who was travelling and questioned them for hours. The patriots looked for the travellers' names in their registers and turned them back, let them pass or stopped them and arrested them in the name of Liberty, Equality, Fraternity, or death[1].

Charles began to realise that there was little chance of his returning to England unless the governors in Paris decided he was a good citizen. He was stopped by patriots twenty times a day. Then, in one small village, he was woken one night by four men wearing red caps. 'You are going to Paris with an escort[2] of three guards, aristocrat[3],' said one. 'You must pay for the escort. You will be arrested when you get to Paris.'

'Thank you, citizen,' said Charles. 'There's nothing I want more than to get to Paris.'

Charles met the three men who were to be his escort. The small group travelled at night and rested during the day. The only time Charles was afraid, was when they came to the town of Beauvais. They arrived in the evening, and the streets were full of people. 'Aristocrat! Aristocrat!' the people called.

'Friends, you are wrong,' said Darnay. 'I am not a traitor.'

The escorts managed to take Darnay to a safe place, where one of

1. Liberty, Equality, Fraternity or death: 自由、平等、友愛或死亡

2. escort: 護送者

3. aristocrat: 貴族

them explained why the people were looking so hard for aristocrats. A new law had been passed: everything belonging to aristocrats now belonged to the state, all aristocrats were to leave France forever and all who returned were to be put to death.

When the people of Beauvais were asleep, Charles and his escort set off on their usual night-time journey. At daylight, they arrived at one of the gates of Paris. The guards at the gate demanded to see the prisoner's papers.

'I am not a prisoner,' said Charles, 'but a free man and a French citizen.'

The head guard told them to wait, while he went into the guard room. Charles Darnay looked around him. He could see that it was easy for people to get into the city, but that it was very difficult to get out. The guards, he noticed, were both patriots and soldiers, but the patriots were the leaders. Many of them, men and women, wore the red cap. The head guard came out of the guard room and told the escort that they could leave.

'Follow me,' the escort said to Darnay.

'Citizen Defarge,' said a man to the head guard, 'is this the aristocrat Evrémonde?'

'This is the man,' said Defarge. 'He uses his mother's name, Darnay.'

'Where is your wife, Evrémonde?' said the man.

'In England.'

'Of course,' replied the man. 'You will go to the prison of La Force.'

'I have committed no crime!' cried Charles.

'We have new laws, Evrémonde, and new crimes, since you were last in France.' He said this with a hard smile. 'Aristocrats have no rights. Take him away, Defarge.'

The man made a note on a piece of paper and handed it to Defarge. Two words were written on the front of the paper: *In Secret*.

Defarge, Charles Darnay and two patriots went down the steps of the guard room and walked into Paris.

'Are you the man who married Doctor Manette's daughter?' asked Defarge, in a low voice.

'Yes,' Charles was surprised.

'My name is Defarge. I have a café near here.'

'My wife came to your house to find her father!' cried Charles.

'Why, in the name of La Guillotine[1], did you come back to Paris?'

'Will you help me, Monsieur Defarge?'

'No, I will not.'

'So am I to be put in prison, without trial, in secret, with no way of communicating with the outside world?'

'You will see. Other people have been buried in other, worse prisons before now.'

'But not by me, Citizen Defarge.'

Defarge looked darkly at him.

'Will you do one thing for me? Will you contact a Mr Lorry from Tellson's Bank and tell him where I am?'

'I will,' said Defarge, 'do *nothing* for you. My duty is to my country and the People.'

As they walked in silence through the streets of Paris, Charles could see how *normal* it was for people to see prisoners walking through the streets. Even the children didn't look at him; it was as

1. La Guillotine: 斷頭台

normal for a man in good clothes to be going to prison as it was for a man in working clothes to be going to work. It was now clear to Charles that he was in great danger: the king was in prison, everyone was talking about how sharp La Guillotine was, and he was about to be locked away *In Secret*.

The prison at La Force was a dark, dirty, poisonous place. Darnay was taken to his cell through the darkness of the prison, through corridors and past rooms full of prisoners. Women were seated at long tables, reading and writing or knitting, while men walked up and down the rooms, talking.

It seemed to Charles Darnay that he was walking through the company of the dead. Ghosts, all of them! The elegant ghost of beauty, the ghost of pride, the ghost of youth, the ghost of age, all waiting to leave this terrible land, eyes changed by the death they had died in coming to this terrible place.

Finally, they came to a single cell. All it contained was a chair, a table and a bed.

'You will be visited,' said the guard as he locked the door and left.

Darnay walked around the cell. He walked round it, measuring the size of his cell and there Charles Darnay was left, as if he were dead.

Stop & Check

1 **Who did these things happen to, or who did these things in Chapter Seven?**

Choose from:

A Mr Lorry
B Jerry Cruncher
C Charles Darnay
D Monsieur Defarge

Which person:

1 ☐ went to France to help Tellson's bank?
2 ☐ pretended to take a letter to the Marquis St. Evrémonde?
3 ☐ went to France to help Mr Lorry?
4 ☐ received a letter from a family employee?
5 ☐ went to Paris in secret?
6 ☐ had difficulty getting to Paris?
7 ☐ did Charles meet in Paris?
8 ☐ refused to help Charles?
9 ☐ was pleased that Charles had been arrested?
10 ☐ was surprised at the attitude of the people of Paris?
11 ☐ met large numbers of prisoners?
12 ☐ was locked away in the prison at La Force?

2 **Answer the questions about Chapter Seven.**

1 Who was the only person in England who knew Charles's real identity?

____

2 Why does Charles feel he has to go back to France?

____

3 How does Dickens describe the prisoners at La Force?

____

4 Why does Dickens say that Charles was 'left, as if he were dead'?

____

Grammar for First

3 Read the text below and think of the word which best fits each gap. Use only one word in each gap.

La Force

La Force was (**1**)_________ of the many prisons in Paris. By the time of the French Revolution, it had only been a prison (**2**)_________ about ten years, having previously been a private house. There were two prisons in the building, one for debtors and one for women who (**3**)_________ been arrested. During the revolution many aristocrats and former governors were held at the prison, although most were moved to another prison, La Conciergerie, before (**4**)_________ execution. Dickens writes about eleven hundred prisoners (**5**)_________ murdered by the mob in the four days that Doctor Manette was away, although it may have been more. More (**6**)_________ a hundred and fifty men and women were killed at La Force. The prison was closed in 1845 and pulled down. Visitors to Paris can (**7**)_________ see the room in La Conciergerie where Queen Marie Antoinette was held before her execution.

Grammar

4a Conditionals. Put the verb in capitals into the correct form to complete the sentences.

1 If I knew the man, I _______________ the letter to him. TAKE

2 Charles wouldn't have gone back to Paris, if Gabelle _______________ to him. NOT WRITE

3 If Charles had stayed in England, Lucie _______________ to Paris. NOT GO

4 If I don't speak to the governors in Paris, I _______________ to go back to London. NOT BE ABLE

5 I would leave Paris, if I _______________ enough money. HAVE

6 He won't help you, if you _______________ an aristocrat. BE

4b Talk in pairs. Discuss what you would do in the following situations.

- If I had the time, ...
- If I had the money, ...

Glossary Work

5a Match the legal word to the definition.

a ☐ treason (n.)
b ☐ court (n.)
c ☐ traitor (n.)
d ☐ witness (n.)
e ☐ give evidence (vb.)
f ☐ jury (n.)

1 to tell a judge what you saw
2 someone who has seen a crime or accident
3 the people who decide whether someone is guilty or innocent
4 a crime against your country
5 a person who has committed a crime against his/her country
6 the building where the judge and jury work

5b Now write a definition for these three words.

g execution (n.) ____________________
h prosecute (vb.) ____________________
i defend (vb.) ____________________

Characters

6a Citizen Defarge. Work in pairs. Think of some examples in *A Tale of Two Cities* of when Defarge has been:

1 very kind to someone ____________________
2 very loyal to someone ____________________
3 very calm ____________________
4 very decisive ____________________
5 very unkind to someone ____________________

6b Do you like Defarge as a character? Why/Why not?

Writing

7 You are Charles Darnay. Write a letter to Lucie from prison Explain:

- what happened to you on your journey to France.
- what your prison is like.
- how you are feeling.

BEFORE-READING ACTIVITY

Listening & Speaking

8a Read this glossary definition from the beginning of Chapter Eight.

grindstone – a type of stone which you can use to make knives and other tools sharp

In pairs, discuss the following questions:

1 Who was using the grindstone?
2 A woman came to see Mr Lorry at Tellson's Bank in Paris. Who?
3 What did the woman tell Mr Lorry?
4 Where is Charles at the moment?
5 Where is Doctor Manette at the moment?

▶ 9 **8b Now listen to the beginning of Chapter Eight and answer the questions. Write your answers below.**

1 ______
2 ______
3 ______
4 ______
5 ______

Chapter Eight

'Save the Prisoner, Evrémonde!'

▶ 9 Tellson's Bank was in the Saint Germain area of Paris, in a house which had belonged to a Monseigneur. Recently, some patriots had placed a large grindstone[1] outside the house, and could now often be seen making their terrible knives sharper on it.

That evening, Mr Lorry was in his office, worrying about the state of the city and considering how much danger Tellson's was in. He heard the sound of the bell at the gate, and glanced at the clock. Who could that be at this time?

Then, there was a sound outside his door, and Mr Lorry's panic was rising as the door opened and Lucie Manette rushed in, followed by her father.

'Lucie! What are you doing here?' was all he could say.

'Charles, Charles is here in Paris! They stopped him at the gates and took him to prison.'

There was the sound of another bell at the gate. Then the sound of footsteps, then the terrible sound of knives against the grindstone.

Doctor Manette walked over to the window.

'No, Manette, don't look,' cried Mr Lorry.

'Mr Lorry,' said the old man, 'don't worry about me. My life's safe in this city. I've been a prisoner in the Bastille. There are no patriots in

1. grindstone: 磨刀石

Paris, or in France, who would touch me. What *is* that noise?'

'Which prison did they take Charles to?' asked Mr Lorry.

'La Force.'

Mr Lorry's eyes fell to the floor. He thought for a minute, then took Lucie out of the room to a smaller one nearby, and asked her to wait for a few minutes. He then went back to his office to tell his terrible news to Doctor Manette.

Doctor Manette was looking out of the window onto the terrible sight of the grindstone below. Forty or fifty men and women were making the executioners' tools sharper. They had swords and knives and the great grindstone was turning, red with blood, like the colour of the wine from the broken barrel, as they made their tools sharp.

'La Force,' said Mr Lorry. 'They are *killing* the prisoners at La Force.

Doctor Manette shook Mr Lorry's hand and said nothing as he opened the door and walked calmly down the stairs to meet the mob. His white hair was flowing behind him and his face was strong and firm. Mr Lorry watched from the window. A few people in the mob stopped to listen to the old man. Then, quietly at first, and then more loudly, they began to shout to the people near the grindstone. 'Help this Bastille prisoner!'

'Save his son! This man spent years in the Bastille!'

'Save the prisoner Evrémonde from La Force!'

The mob moved away from the grindstone, taking Doctor Manette, their new hero, with them.

The following morning, Mr Lorry found a safe place for Lucie Darnay, little Lucie and Miss Pross. He sent Jerry Cruncher with them as an escort, to protect them. By midday, Doctor Manette had still not returned. Mr Lorry waited in his office and, later in the afternoon, he had a visitor. He was a strong, dark-haired man of about forty-five and Mr Lorry knew he had seen this man before.

'Perhaps you remember me from my café?' said Defarge.

'Yes, yes. Do you have a message from Doctor Manette?'

Defarge passed a small piece of paper to Mr Lorry:

Charles is safe, but I can't safely leave him yet. Defarge has a short letter for my daughter. Let him see her.

Mr Lorry was delighted. 'Will you come with me to where Lucie's staying?' he said to Defarge.

'Of course.'

Downstairs, by the terrible grindstone, there were two women: one was knitting.

'Madame Defarge!' cried Mr Lorry, who had last seen her seventeen years before, as she stood knitting. 'Are you coming with us?'

'Yes,' said Defarge. 'She will recognise their faces. It's for their safety, you know.'

Defarge, Mr Lorry, Madame Defarge and her friend, The Vengeance, walked quickly through the streets to where Lucie was staying. Defarge gave her the note from Charles:

My dear Lucie,

I am well, be brave, your father is helping me. Do not try to answer this message, but kiss our daughter for me.

Lucie kissed Defarge's hand, just as she kissed the hand that knitted. The hand that knitted made no response and continued with its work.

'Is this his child?' she asked.

'Yes,' replied Mr Lorry, 'this is Charles's only child.'

'I have seen enough,' said Madame Defarge.

'So, you'll help us?' said Lucie.

Madame Defarge turned to The Vengeance and said, 'We have seen so many women suffer. Husbands, fathers and brothers in prison and worse. Hunger, poverty, death.'

Madame Defarge started knitting again as she walked out of the room. Her shadow remained.

Doctor Manette did not return until four days later. Lucie did not find out until *many* years later that eleven hundred prisoners, women and men, had been killed in those days in Paris prisons, murdered by the mob. The doctor told Mr Lorry everything that he had seen in those last four days: about Darnay, on the list of those waiting for trial; what the judges of the court were like; how some of them were awake during trials and some were asleep.

Mr Lorry was, at first, afraid that the doctor's experiences would cause him to fall ill again. Then, he began to understand that the doctor was strong *because* of those experiences.

Weeks and months passed, and the doctor was now so strong that he was well-respected throughout Paris. His clients included the rich and the poor, the bad and the good, but the doctor used his influence so well that he became the doctor for three prisons, including La Force. Lucie now knew that her husband was no longer alone, but that he was free to talk to other prisoners.

But these were dangerous times: the king was tried[1], found guilty and his head was removed from his body. There was no time for

1. tried: 審判

peace or for pity. Only eight months later, the queen was executed, too. The prisons all over the country were filled with people who had committed no crime, but nobody listened to them. There was one central figure at this terrible time: La Guillotine.

There were jokes about it; the best cure for a headache; it stopped your hair from going grey; it gave you such a fashionably pale face. Yet, it was the sign of the rebirth of the human race. La Guillotine cut off so many heads that it, and the ground that it polluted, turned red forever.

Among these Terrors, Doctor Manette walked, with his head held high. He was sure he could save Lucie's husband. Still, a year and three months had passed and Charles was still in prison. The only good thing was that the doctor was not suspected. He had, after all, been *recalled to life* some eighteen years before.

In all their time in Paris, Lucie had not been sure whether La Guillotine would cut off her husband's head, from one day to another. She threw herself into her daily life. Little Lucie's lessons were always taught; their clothes, always darker than those of their happier London days were always well-kept; the house was always ready to welcome the person who was missing. Sometimes she and her daughter went out for a walk; they had heard that there was a place in Saint Antoine where prisoners at La Force could see people walking. One day they were in that place, when they heard a voice. 'Citizen, where are you going?' the voice said.

The voice had come from a workshop near the street, where a

man was cutting wood (the man who was cutting the wood had once been a mender of roads, but was now a supporter of change).

'Good morning, Citizen,' Lucie said, polite as ever.

In all weathers, snow, wind, rain and sun, Lucie and little Lucie went to walk in the same place, in the hope that Charles would see them. One day, a mob was there, at the scene. People were dancing, hand-in-hand, with The Vengeance. There was no music, just their own singing and no dance could have been as terrible as theirs. Snow fell quietly as Lucie and little Lucie walked to their usual place. This time, the doctor met them at the corner, and just before he spoke, the shadow of Madame Defarge crossed their faces.

'Charles is due in court tomorrow,' said Doctor Manette.

'Tomorrow?' said Lucie.

Liberty, Equality, Fraternity, or death.

◈◈◈

The court of five judges, prosecutor and public jury worked every day. In Darnay's prison, the names of twenty-three prisoners were called, including Charles Evrémonde, known as Darnay. Only twenty were there, as one had died in prison and been forgotten and two had already met La Guillotine and been forgotten. Darnay was desperate: every person he had cared for in prison had been killed by the mob or by La Guillotine.

When Charles Darnay was called, his judges wore rough red caps and the members of the public jury were rough, too. He did not expect a fair trial. The president of the jury wanted to know how long he had lived in England and who he had married. Charles Darnay was happy to tell the court how long and why he had lived in England and that his wife was a Frenchwoman, daughter of Doctor Manette.

The jury liked his answer and some of them were so moved they had tears rolling down their faces, as they heard his story.

'Why didn't you come back to France sooner?' asked the President of the jury.

'I had no money, and I had broken off all relations with my family,' Charles Darnay replied.

The public jury cheered.

Mr Lorry was asked a few questions: the public jury liked him, too. Then Doctor Manette was called and the jury and the crowd could not be silenced. Charles Darnay became a public hero and, for the moment, the crowd had decided. Charles Darnay was to be freed.

He was carried home by an adoring mob, to his Lucie, his little Lucie, to Miss Pross, to Mr Lorry and most of all to Doctor Manette, who allowed himself to be proud of what he had done.

◈◈◈

There was no time to enjoy his freedom: a day later, when Miss Pross and Mr Cruncher had gone shopping, there was a knock at the door. 'Evrémonde?' was the call.

'Who is looking for him?' replied Doctor Manette.

'Patriots!' said a man. 'We know you, Manette, we respect you, but this is the Marquis St. Evrémonde!'

'But on whose orders have you come here?'

'Monsieur and Madame Defarge, Doctor Manette,' said one man. 'And there is another, too. You will find out his name tomorrow.'

Stop & Check

1 Correct the mistakes in Miss Pross's letter to a friend. There are six factual mistakes.

Dearest Miss Jones,
I'm sorry I haven't written for so long. Doctor Manette, Lucie, little Lucie and I are here in an apartment near Barclays Bank in the centre of Paris. A very handsome man called Jerry Cruncher is looking after us for Mr Lorry.
You probably already know that Charles Darnay has been in prison in the Bastille for more than a year! He came to France to help the royal family and now he needs help himself. Doctor Manette is doing very well, he is a well-respected shoemaker in Paris.
Charles has not yet been tried in court, we expect this to happen at any time and we are afraid that the court could send him back to England.
I'll write again as soon as I can,
Your friend,
Miss Pross

Vocabulary

2 Look again at the first page of Chapter Eight. Find words that mean the same as the words/phrases below. The words are in the same order in the text.

1 put ____________

2 anxious ____________

3 thinking about ____________

4 increasing ____________

5 hurried ____________

6 horrible ____________

3 **Use of English. Complete the second sentence so that it has a similar meaning to the first sentence, using the word given. Do not change the word given. You must use between two and five words, including the word given.**

1 Charles went to France in spite of the danger.

ALTHOUGH

Charles went to ....

2 She won't be able to get there, if she doesn't leave early.

UNLESS

She won't be able to get there ....

3 'Why did she come back to Paris?'

SHE

He asked .... to Paris.

4 Where's the prison?'

WONDERED

She ....

5 The patriots are asking him questions at the moment.

INTERVIEWED

He .... the patriots at the moment.

6 She started to visit him a year ago.

VISITING

She .... a year.

7 Why did you permit him to come to Paris?

LET

Why .... to Paris?

8 I've never seen such a bad thing.

EVER

This is the .... seen.

9 `They're killing the prisoners at La Force.'

BEING

The prisoners at La Force ....

Writing & Speaking

4a Who says these things in Chapter Eight?

1 'Charles, Charles is in Paris!'

____

2 'I've been a prisoner in the Bastille.'

____

3 'Perhaps you remember me from my café?'

____

4 'We have seen so many women suffer.'

____

5 'Why didn't you come back to France sooner?'

____

6 'I had broken off all relations with my family.'

____

7 'On whose orders have you come here?'

____

4b Work in pairs and discuss your answers to these questions.

1 Was Lucie right to come to Paris?
2 Why does Madame Defarge want to see Lucie?
3 How important is Mr Lorry to the story?

Word-building

5 The words in the box are all nouns. Make an adjective from them for each sentence below.

influence • hunger • pollution • politeness • pride

1 Doctor Manette was __________ of his actions.
2 Bread was expensive and people were __________.
3 The streets of the city were __________.
4 Doctor Manette was becoming __________.
5 Lucie was always __________ to the mender of roads.

Characters

6a Work in pairs. Make notes about how these characters have changed throughout *A Tale of Two Cities*.

1 Doctor Manette

2 Charles Darnay

3 Madame Defarge

6b Do you think Lucie has changed? Why and how?/Why not?

Speaking

7a Here are some facts about the final chapter of *A Tale of Two Cities*. Discuss them in pairs.

1 Sydney Carton comes to Paris. Why?
2 A letter from Doctor Manette is read at Darnay's second trial. What does it say?
3 Someone is sentenced to be executed? Who?
4 Madame Defarge has a secret. What is it?
5 An important female character is killed. Who?
6 An important male character is killed. Who?

7b Now read the final chapter and find out!

Chapter Nine

A Life You Love

▶ 10 It was a cold night and, after their shopping, Miss Pross and Jerry Cruncher were walking quickly back to the Darnay family home, when they met a very familiar face. 'Mr Carton!' said Miss Pross. 'We are so pleased to see you!'

'I'm here for one reason,' said Sydney Carton, 'I'm here to help Charles.'

The next day, brought the second trial of Charles Darnay, and Sydney Carton was there to see it. Mr Lorry was there, as were Lucie and her father.

'Charles Evrémonde, also known as Darnay, Aristocrat, Public Enemy,' said one of the judges.

'Who has accused him?'

'Ernest Defarge, owner of a café.'

'Good.'

'Thérèse Defarge, his wife.'

'Good.'

'Alexandre Manette, doctor.'

There was a loud shout from the court. Doctor Manette rose to his feet. 'I have not accused this man! He is my son-in-law!'

'Calm down, citizen Manette,' said the judge, 'I'm sure there will be some reason for this.'

Defarge was the first to speak. He explained how he knew Doctor Manette (he had been a servant in the Manette house as a young man) and how he had visited One Hundred and Five North Tower on the day the Bastille had been taken. He produced a document which had been written by the doctor and hidden in his cell.

'Read the document to the court!' ordered the President of the jury.

I, Alexandre Manette, unfortunate doctor, am writing this true story in my prison cell in the Bastille in December, 1767. I will hide this in the wall of my cell, and perhaps someone, one day, will read this sad story. I have been in this terrible prison for ten years now, and I know I will die here.

One cloudy night in December, 1757, I was walking by the river in Paris, when a carriage with two noblemen stopped and asked me to come and care for a person who was ill. I agreed. I got into their carriage and we drove to a house in the countryside. The servant at the house was slow to answer the door and one of the two noblemen hit him across the face when he finally came. I hated to see them treat a man like a dog. They took off their coats and I could see that they were twin brothers. They took me upstairs to my patient, a beautiful young woman, not much older than twenty. She had a very high temperature and all she did was count to twelve and repeat these words, 'My husband, my father, and my brother!'

The two noblemen said the woman had been in this condition since the night before, and that there was another patient who needed my attention. He was in a room nearby and he was a handsome boy of about seventeen – clearly poor. I could see that he was dying and the cause of his near death was an injury[1] from a knife or sword. He didn't want me to examine him, so I asked the noblemen what had happened.

1. **injury:** 受傷、傷口

'This servant forced my brother to use his sword,' he said, with no pity in his voice.

The boy's eyes had moved to the noblemen while he spoke and now they moved back to me. 'Doctor, they're very proud men; they steal from us, they hit us and sometimes they kill us. She ... have you seen her, doctor? She's my sister. They used her, as they use so many. They think it's their right.

Then, the boy, with a great effort, pointed his finger at the noblemen, 'Those men took her away and kept her here, a prisoner. My father died of a broken heart. I have another sister, I took her away to a safe place, far away from these men. Then, I came here, last night. He threw me some money. Money! I attacked him and he, he killed me. She saw it, my sister saw it all.'

The boy was dying. 'Marquis!' he said, 'May God punish you and all your evil family, every last member of your evil family.'

Those were his final words. The boy lay dead. I went back to his sister, whose condition had not changed,

'My husband, my father, and my brother! One, two, three, four, five, six, seven, eight, nine, ten, eleven, twelve.'

The sister survived for a week, getting weaker and weaker all the time. When she died, the noblemen offered me money, which, of course, I refused to take.

I returned home, to my lovely wife, although I told her nothing.

I decided to write a letter to the Minister giving all the details of the case. I thought that the noblemen would probably escape justice, but I felt better writing the letter. I had just finished writing, when a lady came to see me. She introduced herself as the wife of the Marquis St. Evrémonde and she had her very young son, Charles, with her. She told me she knew about her husband's evil treatment of the woman and her family, she knew that there was a sister and that she wanted to help that sister. I now knew the name of the noblemen, but I didn't know the name of the poor woman's sister.

When the lady had left, I added the name Evrémonde to my letter and took it to the Minister myself. Later that evening, Ernest Defarge answered a ring at the door. He showed a man into my study. The man told me that there was an urgent medical case, and would I please come with him in his carriage. That carriage brought me here, to this prison, where the Marquis and his evil brother were waiting. The Marquis had my letter in his hands and burned it in front of me. I was put in this cell, here in my living grave. I don't know what has happened to my wife, whether she's alive or dead. I, Alexandre Manette, unhappy prisoner, accuse the Evrémonde family in Heaven and on earth.

Once the letter had been read, the whole courtroom called for the blood of Evrémonde. It was clear that the Defarges had found the letter with other documents in the Bastille and had kept it, to use it when they wanted. It was clear that the name of Evrémonde had always been on the register at Saint Antoine and that nothing could ever remove it. It was also clear that, by accusing the Evrémonde family so many years ago, Doctor Manette had caused the death of his son-in-law. Madame Defarge smiled at The Vengeance as the sentence came: execution in twenty-four hours.

◈◈◈

Lucie felt dead inside as she heard the sentence. She asked for, and was given, permission to speak to her husband one last time. Her father, running his fingers through his white hair, tried to get onto his knees in front of Darnay.

'No, sir, get up, don't!' cried Darnay. 'Good could never come from such evil as the Evrémonde family had in their hearts!'

Darnay was taken out of the prisoners' door and Lucie fainted at her father's feet. Carton picked her up and carried her to his carriage and escorted the Manettes home. He was calm and determined. 'Doctor Manette, you must try again. The judges listened to you before, they may listen to you again.'

'Yes, I'll try. I may still have some influence, because of my days at the Bastille.' The old man left.

Mr Lorry was sure there was nothing they could do except try to get Lucie and her daughter safely out of Paris. 'I'm afraid he'll die,' he whispered to Carton.

'I agree,' echoed Sydney Carton. 'There will be an execution tomorrow.' He kissed Lucie goodbye and, as he left, he whispered, 'A life you love.'

Sydney Carton was decisive and brave. He walked into Defarge's café. Madame Defarge and her husband were there and she looked suspiciously at him. For a moment, she even thought he was Darnay. Sydney ordered a drink in very bad French, and pulled out an English newspaper. Madame Defarge continued her conversation with her two companions, The Vengeance and Jacques Three. 'I have seen her, and her daughter,' whispered Madame Defarge, 'and their names are on the register.' She pointed at her knitting.

The Vengeance wanted to add her own opinion, 'Then there's Doctor Manette, a man of such influence!'

'We can stop at Evrémonde, my dear,' said Defarge to his wife.

'You would let him go, even now!' she replied.

'Kill them all!' said Jacques Three.

'Yes,' said Madame Defarge, 'and there is one thing you do not know. I knew, I have always known. The Evrémondes are evil, evil for what they did to my family. Yes, *my* family. The poor girl in Manette's letter was my sister. *They* killed my sister, my brother and my father, and no, I will not rest until *his* wife, *their* daughter and the old man follow the last of the Evrémonde line to La Guillotine.'

Some customers came into the shop, giving Sydney Carton the chance to leave in order to warn Mr Lorry that Lucie, her daughter and her father had to leave Paris immediately. When he reached Mr Lorry's office, Sydney realised that Doctor Manette had not yet returned. They set out to look for him. Around midnight, the two men found him wandering around the streets in the area, looking for his shoemaker's bench. Sydney knew that there was only one thing to do. He pulled out his passport and handed it to Mr Lorry. 'I've decided to speak to Charles tomorrow at the prison. Please, keep this safe for me,' he said. 'I think we should all leave Paris tomorrow at two. They won't come for Lucie and the child immediately. They will wait until the crowd has finished celebrating. We must go immediately after the execution, if we are to escape.'

'You're right, Carton,' said Mr Lorry. 'You're a fine man: clear-thinking and intelligent.'

'You must promise one thing. As soon as I come to you tomorrow at two, take me, Lucie and her daughter immediately to England and ask no questions.'

'I will, I will. I'll be proud to have you at my side,' said Mr Lorry.

⬥⬥⬥

Charles had spent the night writing letters to Lucie, Doctor Manette, his daughter and Mr Lorry. He knew he was going to die. He had counted the hours all night and all morning: nine, gone forever, ten, gone forever, until one o'clock came, and with it came Sydney Carton.

'Quick man, take off your boots and put mine on,' said Carton.

'No, no. I can never escape from here. Don't add your execution to mine!'

Carton had no time to waste. He placed a bottle under Charles Darnay's nose and Darnay fell to the ground. Taking off his coat and boots, Carton dressed Darnay to look like himself. He then tied back his own hair and called the guards. 'This man has no stomach for[1] prisons! I believe his carriage is outside.'

The guards laughed as they carried Darnay to Carton's carriage and laughed again as they came back a few minutes later to take *Carton* to meet *Darnay's* appointment with La Guillotine.

Just before two o'clock that afternoon, Mr Lorry, Lucie Darnay, little Lucie and Doctor Manette got into their carriage with the half-conscious figure of Charles Darnay and drove through the gates of Paris.

At the same time as the Darnays were leaving Paris, and as Sydney Carton was making his way to La Guillotine, Madame Defarge was making her way to Lucie's home in Paris. 'The Evrémonde family must be executed, and that includes his wife and child.'

She opened the door, walked calmly into the apartment and looked

1. has no stomach for: 沒有膽量

around. There, in front of three closed doors stood Miss Pross, alone. Jerry had gone to find a carriage so that they could meet up with Mr Lorry, before taking the boat for England. He had promised to give up his night-time '*fishing*' for bodies to sell, if only the Manettes got back to England in safety and was even hoping that his wife *was* praying for him and for them. Jerry's hands were now completely clean.

'Where is the wife of Evrémonde?' cried Madame Defarge, staring at the three closed doors.

Miss Pross stood, with her arms folded. Neither woman understood the other's language, but still they spoke to each other, and both understood the importance of the moment. 'Every minute I can delay you increases my dear girl's chances of escape!' said Miss Pross.

'I demand to see her, now!' cried Madame Defarge, throwing open one of the doors. 'They've gone!' she cried. 'Get out of the way!' and Madame Defarge took the gun from her belt and ran at Miss Pross.

Miss Pross was too strong, the gun went off with a terrible bang and there, on the floor, lay Madame, dead. Miss Pross ran to where she had planned to meet Mr Cruncher. She couldn't answer any of his concerned questions, because she couldn't hear them. Deaf, from that terrible bang of the gun, Miss Pross never heard anything again.

Along the streets of Paris, the death-carts travelled. In the third cart came a man, holding the hand of a young servant. They didn't know each other, but were united now, in the moments before their deaths.

'Which one is Evrémonde?' called one of the crowd.

'The one holding the girl's hand!'

They had reached the place with La Guillotine. There was a line of chairs at the front, where women sat knitting red caps. One chair was empty and The Vengeance was standing near it, calling for her friend Thérèse Defarge, who never normally missed an execution.

The man they thought was Evrémonde got out of the cart, helping the poor servant girl. 'Just look at me and think about me,' he said as she climbed the stairs in front of him.

They said about him, in the city that night, that no man ever had a more peaceful expression on his face as he got ready for his execution. He had been thinking about the happy peaceful lives of those he was dying to save. One thought passed through Sydney Carton's head as his turn came to climb the steps. 'It is a far, far better thing that I do than I have ever done; it is a far, far better rest that I go to than I have ever known.'

Stop & Check

1 Discuss the questions below in pairs. Write your answers in the spaces below.

1 How had Doctor Manette accused his son-in-law?

____

2 How were the twin brothers in the doctor's letter related to Charles Darnay?

____

3 What was the relationship between the poor woman in the doctor's letter and Madame Defarge?

____

4 Why had Doctor Manette been sent to prison at the Bastille?

____

5 What did Mr Lorry think would happen to Charles Darnay?

____

6 How did Charles Darnay escape from prison?

____

7 Who killed Madame Defarge?

____

8 Why did Miss Pross go deaf?

____

9 How did Sydney Carton feel when he went to La Guillotine?

____

2 Look at Sydney Carton's final words before his execution.

'It is a far, far better thing that I do than I have ever done; it is a far, far better rest that I go to than I have ever known.'

Talk in pairs.

1 What exactly does he mean by *thing*?

2 What exactly does he mean by *rest*?

Speaking

3 Work in pairs. Discuss your answers and give reasons for them.

1. What did you think of the ending of *A Tale of Two Cities*?
2. Did you like the way the story moved between Paris and London?
3. In one film version, Sydney Carton is saved at the end. Do you think a happier ending would have been better or worse?
4. Why had Madame Defarge become so hard? Did you feel sorry for her?
5. Did you enjoy the novel? Why?/Why not?

Writing

4 You recently saw this notice in an English-language magazine called *Literature Today*. Use the answers you discussed in exercise 3 to help you.

Reviews needed!

Have you read a novel recently? If so, we want your review. All you need to do is give an overview of the story you have read. Then, tell us about the characters and the setting and say whether you would recommend the story to other people or not.

The best reviews will appear on the magazine website!

Write your review in 120–180 words.

Charles Dickens (1812 – 1870)

Charles Dickens is one of the most important English writers. He wrote a large number of novels, but he also wrote short stories, essays, newspaper articles and travel books. He is regarded by many as one of the finest writers of the Victorian Age.

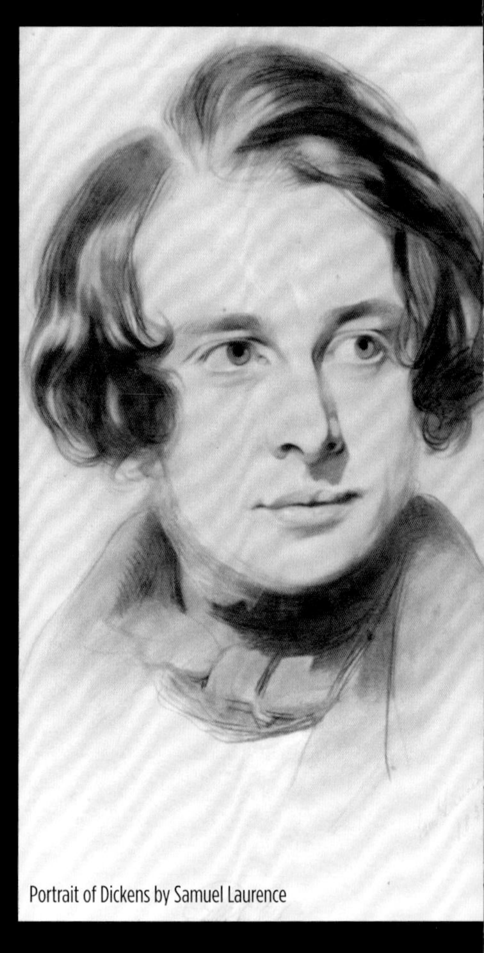
Portrait of Dickens by Samuel Laurence

Early Life

Charles John Huffam Dickens was born in Landport, Portsmouth on the south coast of England, on February 7th 1812. He was the second of eight children. His father, John Dickens, was a secretary. Charles' mother's name was Elizabeth.

When Charles was four years old, the family moved to Chatham in Kent. Charles was very happy there. His father paid for him to go to a private school, which he liked very much.

In 1822, his father began to experience financial problems, so the family moved to London. They lived in Camden Town, a poor area of London, and they could no longer afford to send their children to school.

Money Problems

In Victorian times, people often went to debtors' prison if they had financial problems. In 1824, John Dickens and his family (as was common at the time) went to prison for debt. Rather than join them in prison, Charles started work in a factory to try and help his family. His life was very hard and he often wrote about child labour, prisons and factory conditions in his work. When the family came out of prison, Charles went back to school. He studied until he was fifteen years old, then he started work.

Work and Family

Charles' first job was in a lawyer's office. Then he worked for a newspaper and as a reporter for parliament. He started writing short stories at the same time. In 1833, a magazine called the *Monthly Magazine* published Charles' first short story, *A Dinner at Poplar Walk*. In 1836, he published his first book *Sketches by Boz*. He used the name Boz as a nickname for many years. In the same year, he married Catherine Hogarth, the daughter of a newspaper editor. Together, they had ten children, although the marriage was unhappy and they eventually separated when Dickens was writing *A Tale of Two Cities*.

1836 Dickens' first book *Sketches by Boz*

Dickens' Interests

Charles never forgot his early days, especially the time when he was poor. He spent a lot of his later years fighting for social change. He wrote a lot of newspaper articles attacking poverty and social conditions, and novels, such as *Oliver Twist*, shocked his readers. One of his Christmas stories, *A Christmas Carol*, has a powerful message about poverty. *A Tale of Two Cities* is different from many of his other novels, most of which had relied on characterisation rather than plot. Some critics were disappointed at this change, but Dickens himself called it 'the best story I have written'.

Final Days

At the beginning of June 1870, Charles became very ill, and died on June 9th. He is buried in Poets' Corner – a part of Westminster Abbey, London – a great honour for a writer.

Task

Complete the form with the information about the author.

Full Name: ____________________

Date of Birth: ____________________

Place of Birth: ____________________

Parents' Names: ____________________

Wife's Name: ____________________

Children: ____________________

Four Important Works: ____________________

Date of Death: ____________________

The French Revolution – Important Events

Many people think that the French Revolution started and ended in 1789 but, of course, things were much more complicated than that and the period of revolution was much longer.

Before 1789

By the time Louis XIV became king in 1775, France was already experiencing financial problems, which only got worse as France invested money in the American Revolution and its consequent wars. Things got even more difficult in 1788, when there was severe weather, meaning that there was very little food, especially in Paris, which was already a very large city. This, combined with the government and king's need for more money, began to convince Louis that it was a good idea to recall some older institutions such as *parlement* (parliament) and the *Estates-General* (church, noblemen and some representatives of the middle classes).

1789: the Great Fear and the Storming of the Bastille

Louis recalled the Estates-General in 1789, making people believe that some change was coming, although most members of these political classes had no real interest in social change. There was a demand from some areas of the church, and some other members of the middle classes, for a National Assembly and this gained popular support. A rumour, called the Great Fear, started immediately after Louis agreed to a National Assembly. The fear was that Louis's army was waiting to come into Paris, and this led to the attack by patriots on the Bastille.

The Assembly

The National Assembly was quick to pass a Declaration of Rights which included Liberty, Equality, Fraternity. Soon, land belonging to the church became public property and a new constitution was written. King Louis and his family 'moved' to Paris and were effectively under the control of the Assembly. They were put in prison in 1792, when the Assembly became more radical.

The Execution of Louis XIV and the Reign of Terror

In 1793, the king was executed, as revolutionary wars spread. There was unrest in many areas of France, because of lack of food and inflation. The National Assembly became the National Convention and the revolutionaries began to execute large numbers of people they accused of being against Public Safety. Attempts to improve the supply of food to Paris caused problems in other areas of France.

The Directory and Napoleon Bonaparte

There were a number of pro-revolution and anti-revolution attempts at government, but they ended when a government of five (the Directory) was set up. This also failed, and ended when Napoleon took power, abolished the Directory and effectively became a dictator.

Task

How much do you know about the American Revolution?

1 When did it start?

a ☐ 1775 **b** ☐ 1789

c ☐ 1765

2 How many colonies first declared independence?

a ☐ 51 **b** ☐ 25

c ☐ 13

3 Who were the colonies separating from?

a ☐ France **b** ☐ England

c ☐ Spain

4 When did it end?

a ☐ 1783 **b** ☐ 1789

c ☐ 1792

FOCUS ON...

Rich and Poor in France and England

Charles Dickens was writing at a time when the threat of revolution in England was still very real. Having been poor himself and his father having been in debt, Dickens had a great deal of sympathy with those who called for social change. It is clear from the picture he paints of Madame Defarge, however, that he was concerned about the cruel, violent face of revolution.

The Aristocracy

Dickens takes the view, not held by many historians today, that the main causes of the French Revolution were bad government of the country by noblemen and high, unfair taxation placed on poorer people. The causes were more complex, although the court of King Louis XIV was a symbol of wealth and excess. The situation was more contained in England, probably because the aristocrats in the government recognised the danger and reacted more quickly to ideas for wider democracy.

The Middle Classes

The middle classes were mainly those who carried out everyday government in the towns and cities of both France and England. People would be well-educated, often wealthy and would have a certain amount of power. Those who came from families who had earned money through trade were not always welcome in higher social circles, although as the aristocracy got poorer, this changed. The middle classes were generally more in favour of liberal ideas in both France and England in Dickens' time.

Prince Albert, Queen Victoria's husband

Poverty

There were many problems caused by poverty in the late eighteenth and early nineteenth centuries. In France, at the time of the Revolution, there had been terrible problems with agriculture because of bad land management by the owners and because of problems with weather. Hunger was as common in England and other parts of the British Isles. There were illnesses caused by drinking dirty water or eating dirty food, especially in the new industrial cities, where most people were poor. It's a mistake to think that rich people didn't have any problems: Prince Albert, Queen Victoria's husband, died of typhoid. Taxes were more of a problem in France, where the system was still feudal (the owners, like the Monseigneurs in *A Tale of Two Cities* had a great degree of control over the lives of the people who lived on their land).

The Condition of Children

It was completely normal for children from poor families to work; it was even thought that work was good for children. This was widespread in agriculture as well as in industry: child workers were very cheap and there were lots of them. Children often started work when they were four or five years old. Dickens himself had worked from a young age and the condition of children is a recurrent theme in *A Tale of Two Cities* as in many of Dickens' novels.

Task
Internet Research.

Were there great differences in social classes in your city at any time in its history? Find some facts on the Internet and write a paragraph about rich and poor.

Crime and Punishment

France and Britain, as can be seen from *A Tale of Two Cities*, both had cruel punishments for those who were found guilty of a crime.

Physical and Capital Punishment

Unlike in many countries today, it was common for people who had committed a crime to be punished physically and in other cases, for criminals to be killed. France first used the guillotine during the revolution to kill people, although a similar machine had been used in other European countries. It was considered a quicker and more efficient way of killing noblemen and women, who would previously have been killed by a sword. The guillotine remained in use in France until the twentieth century. The last person to be killed by the guillotine in France, Hamida Djandoubi, died in 1977. In Britain, hanging was the most common form of execution.

Prisons

In the eighteenth and nineteenth century, prisons were terrible, just as they are in many places today. Charles Dickens often wrote about the conditions at Newgate Prison: the largest prison in London, where people had to cook, wash, live and sleep in a very small area. There were often different sections in prisons: a section for men, a section for debtors (like the original use of La Force in Paris) and a section for women and children. Dickens uses *A Tale of Two Cities* to compare being in prison to being buried.

Newgate Prison

HMS York (1807) as a prison ship

Crimes against Travellers

Travellers were especially afraid of violent crime. As can be seen from the first chapter of *A Tale of Two Cities*, people who travelled on the roads were terrified of robbers (called highwaymen) who waited with guns and knives to steal valuables from them. This type of crime was common world-wide and was punished with the death penalty in most countries. Highwaymen and robbers were often heroes (to people who didn't travel) and people wrote songs and ballads about them. Pickpockets, or cutpurses (people kept their money in purses attached to their bodies with strings), were common in towns and cities.

Transportation

One normal punishment in Dickens' times was transportation to a different country. Britain sent people to Australia and Tasmania and to America. This changed after the American Declaration of Independence. More than 160,000 people were transported to Australia in about eighty years. They were men, women and children, but the majority were men. Of course, the journeys across the ocean were very hard and dangerous: prison ships were always old and in poor condition. Sometimes people stayed on the ships for more than a year. In the 1850s, transportation to Australia finally stopped. France began transporting prisoners towards the end of the nineteenth century: Alfred Dreyfus is probably the most famous person to have been transported from France.

Task

Do some Internet research about crime and punishment in your city. Write a paragraph about it and compare it with conditions today.

TEST YOURSELF 自測

Glossary Crossword. How many words can you remember from the glossary of *A Tale of Two Cities*? Use the clues to complete the crossword.

Clues Across

2 A place in the ground where you bury a dead person. (5 letters)
4 A room in a prison. (4 letters)
6 A lawyer who tries to show that a person is guilty. (10 letters)
9 The person who does this is a traitor, and the crime is _____ . (7 letters)
10 A violent and angry crowd of people. (3 letters)
11 A large container for liquid. (6 letters)

Clues Down

1 A person who goes with you to protect you or look after you. (6 letters)
3 A repetition of a sound in the air. The sound hits something and then comes back to you. (4 letters)
5 A group of people who listen to a trial and decide if a person is guilty or innocent. (4 letters)
7 You do this when you make food or drink go from your mouth into your stomach. (7 letters)
8 To put someone's name onto an official list. Also the list itself. (8 letters)

SYLLABUS 語法重點和學習主題

Level B2

This reader contains the items listed below, as well as those included in previous levels of the ELI Readers syllabus.

Verbs:
present perfect continuous
past perfect continuous
perfect infinitives
a variety of phrasal verbs
complex passive forms
wish/if only
modal verbs: might, needn't
reporting verbs: explain, repeat, reply, answer, ask, cry, scream, shout
tenses with *This is the first ...*

Types of Clause:
type-three conditionals
mixed conditionals
relative: embedded, defining

Other:
connectives: although, despite, in spite of, however
time sequencers
inversion

A Tale of Two Cities

pp6 & 7

1 1 B was 2 C actually 3 A title 4 D over 5 D reflecting 6 B marriage 7 A remains

2 1 asked 2 screamed 3 replied 4 answered 5 cried 6 shouted 7 whispered

3 Various answers are possible.

4

death	robbery
funeral	passenger
young	king
elderly	punishment
prisoner	crime
nervous	gun

pp16-19

1 1 The mail coach was travelling to Dover.
2 A man on a horse stopped the coach.
3 He handed over a message to one of the travellers, a Mr Lorry.
4 Mr Lorry then gave a message for the man to take to Tellson's Bank.
5 The Coach finally arrived at The George Hotel in Dover.
6 Mr Lorry asked a servant there to tell him as soon as a lady called Miss Manette arrived.
7 When the lady arrived, she asked to speak to Mr Lorry immediately.
8 Mr Lorry told her that her father was still alive.
9 Miss Manette felt faint and a lady with a red face looked after her.

2 1 look forward to 2 ruled 3 sure 4 hard 5 quietly 6 afraid 7 terrible 8 murder 9 common

3a 1 It was the season of darkness, but also the season of light.
2 It was the age of wisdom, but also the age ofstupidity.
3 It was the spring of hope, it was the winter of despair.
4 There was a justice system, but it was known for its cruelty.
5 People in Paris and in London suffered in poverty.
6 The courts didn't seem to be able to tell the difference between a thief and a murderer.
7 Secrecy is important to this mission.
8 You must bring your father back to health.

3b Various answers are possible.

4 Various answers are possible.

5 1 She had never been to Paris before.
FIRST
It was the first time she had ever been to Paris.
2 It was only because the coach had stopped that the messenger caught them.
NEVER
If the coach hadn't stopped, the messenger would never have caught them.
3 Mr Lorry advised Miss Manette to look after her father.
WERE
'If I were you, I would look after your father,' Mr Lorry said.
4 The horses couldn't pull the coach up the hill because it was too steep.
MUCH
The hill was much too steep for the horses.
5 I wish I had known that my father was alive!
ONLY
If only I had known that my father was alive.
6 'She has arrived from London,' said the waiter to him.
TOLD
The waiter told him she had arrived from London.

7 They decided to stay in the hotel, because there was a chance of rain.
CASE
They decided to stay in the hotel in case it rained.

8 'I'd prefer to get a boat in the morning.'
RATHER
I'd rather get a boat in the morning.

6 Various answers are possible.

7a

1 narrow	B	6 steady	P
2 strong	B	7 elderly	B
3 curly	B	8 poor	N
4 faint	B	9 steep	B
5 round	B	10 poisonous	N

7b Various answers are possible.

pp 28-31

1

1 B Madame Defarge	7 C Doctor Manette
2 D Mr Lorry	8 C Doctor Manette
3 B Madame Defarge	9 D Mr Lorry
4 D Mr Lorry	10 C Doctor Manette
5 D Mr Lorry	11 C Doctor Manette
6 A Lucie	12 B Madame Defarge

2 1 Red.
2 Possible answer: To burn for warmth.
3 Hard, cold reality. Hunger, cold, illness, work.
4 Possible answer: It's the colour of blood.

3 1 reality 2 fault 3 anger 4 poverty 5 atmosphere 6 surprise
7 pride 8 recognition 9 confusion

R							P			S
	E	A	N	G	E	R	O			U
F		C	C				V			R
A	T	M	O	S	P	H	E	R	E	P
U			N	G			R			R
L			F		N		T			I
T	P		U			I	Y			S
		R	S				T			E
			I	R	E	A	L	I	T	Y
			O	D					O	
			N		E					N

4a overcrowding, lots of rubbish, extreme poverty, bad air

4b Various answers are possible.

5 Various answers are possible.

6 1 barrel jar bottle glass
Various answers are possible.
2 elderly old ancient young
Various answers are possible.
3 icy freezing cold warm
Various answers are possible.
4 shoe boot cap sandal
Various answers are possible.
5 toe finger arm hand
Various answers are possible.

7a Various answers are possible.

7b
1 steel
2 wooden
3 plastic
4 large
5 dark
6 old-fashioned
7 small
8 ugly
9 spacious
10 beautiful
11 comfortable
12 old
13 damp
14 modern

pp 40-43

1 Suggested answers
1 What differences are there between Jerry Cruncher and his son, young Jerry Cruncher?
Age.
2 Why do you think Jerry Cruncher was concerned about going into the court?
Probably because it was the first time he'd been in a court.
3 Why do you think people paid to go into courts at the time?
For entertainment.
4 Describe the young man who was on trial.
25 years old, tall and good-looking, tanned with dark eyes, hair tied back, calm and respectful.
5 Why do you think the people in the court are described as buzzing like flies?
Because of the noise they make when chatting. You find flies around the body of a dead person.
6 Do you think that Barsad and Cly were honest?
Various answers are possible.
7 Why do you think Darnay was found innocent?
Various answers are possible.
8 Why was Doctor Manette so different now?
He was away from his prison with his daughter.
9 What impression did Darnay make on Miss Manette?
She felt pity for him.
10 Why do you think Sydney Carton was so bitter?
He was jealous that Miss Manette paid attention to Darnay.

2 1 Prosecutor 2 Defence lawyer 3 Judge 4 Doorman

3 Tyburn was a terrible place (1) near/in London where criminals were hanged in (2) the past. It is very near to the area (3) of Marble Arch and the first hanging of a criminal there probably dates (4) back to the twelfth century. The early executions at Tyburn were almost (5) always public, as it wasn't until much later when executions were held in private. The place where people were hanged at Tyburn was, in later centuries, (6) called Tyburn Tree, and more than one person could be hanged at the same time. Public hangings were popular events; almost (7) always public holidays. The youngest person to (8) be executed at Tyburn was probably under the age of fourteen. The largest number of people who ever went to watch a public execution is thought to be about 200,000. The last person to face execution (9) at Tyburn was a man who had been found guilty of robbing people on a mail coach – just as the travellers feared (10) in Chapter One of *A Tale of Two Cities*.

4 Various answers are possible.

5a 5b and **5c** Various answers are possible.

6a 1 keen on 2 interested in 3 suspected of 4 guilty of 5 bored by 6 good at

6b Various answers are possible.

7a 7b Various answers are possible.

pp 52-55

1 Miss Manette and her father are now living in a quiet street in the centre of London. Mr Lorry, Sydney Carton and Charles Darnay sometimes visit them. One day, Doctor Manette gets very upset when he hears about something hidden by a prisoner in the Tower of London.
In Paris, the Marquis St. Evrémonde's carriage kills a child by driving too fast. When he returns to his castle, we find out that he is waiting for his nephew, Charles Darnay, to arrive from England. Charles tells him that he no longer wants to live in France and that he has decided to live in England. The Marquis asks whether Charles knows Doctor Manette and his daughter. That night, the Marquis St. Evrémonde is killed with a knife while he's sleeping.

2 Dickens believed that the French Revolution was caused by the (1) wealthy aristocrats and governors of France. He believed that the revolution became inevitable, as the (2) poverty of the majority of the population was ignored. The behaviour of the local (3) noblemen, or Monseigneurs, is contrasted with the lives of the (4) poor. The Marquis St. Evrémonde is an arrogant example of a Monseigneur: he treats his (5) servants badly. The villagers who live on his land have to pay (6) taxes to him, even though they are poor and hungry.

3a 3b Various answers are possible.

4a
1 turn off — b stop something from working
2 take off — f remove
3 set off — d start
4 keep off — e not go somewhere
5 go off — a go bad
6 wear off — c stop having an effect

4b
1 We set off late, so we missed the plane.
2 You should always turn off the TV when you leave a room.
3 Keep off the grass!
4 The aspirin's worn off, I think I'll take another.
5 It smells terrible, I think the milk has gone off.
6 Take off your coat! It's hot in here.

5 Chocolate is (1) made from cacao beans and most cacao is grown in Africa, although the cacao tree (2) actually originated in the Americas. The Aztecs and Mayans both used cacao in bitter drinks, (3) unlike the Europeans, who added sugar and milk to (4) sweeten it, when chocolate was introduced in the sixteenth century. Chocolate is thought to have a (5) powerful effect on serotonin levels in the brain and (6) researchers are currently working to (7) identify other positive and negative effects. It is poisonous to some animals, (8) including mice, rats, cats and dogs. Chocolate is (9) commonly added to cakes and biscuits in many parts of the world and in Europe and the United States, excessive (10) consumption may have increased obesity rates.

6 Various answers are possible.

7a 1 *un*comfortable 2 irrelevant 3 illogical 4 unfortunate 5 inedible 6 irregular 7 illiterate 8 unconscious 9 impatient

7b
1 The prisoner was not a lucky man. The prisoner was unfortunate.
2 Many of the poor couldn't read or write. They were illiterate.
3 The Marquis couldn't wait to get home. He was impatient.

8
1 What is Darnay now doing?
a Teaching French in England.
b Teaching English in France.
c Looking for a job with the government.

2 How does Darnay feel about Lucie Manette?
a He likes her, but is in love with someone else.
b He likes her, but hopes she will marry Sydney Carton.
c He loves her, and wants to marry her.

3 Someone else has recently visited Lucie. Who is it?
a Mr Lorry.
b Sydney Carton.
c John Barsad, the spy.

4 Why doesn't Darnay tell Doctor Manette his real name?
a Doctor Manette doesn't want to know his real name.
b Darnay doesn't want anyone to know his real name.
c Darnay is afraid that Sydney Carton will steal his identity.

pp 64-67

1
1 Charles Darnay tells Doctor Manette that he wants to marry Lucie.
2 Sydney Carton tells Lucie that he's in love with her.
3 Jerry Cruncher goes to a funeral.
4 Jerry Cruncher's son sees his father digging up a body.
5 The mender of roads tells everyone in the café about Gaspard's death.
6 We find out why Madame Defarge knits so much.
7 Lucie and Charles get married.

8 Lucie and Charles go on their honeymoon.
9 Doctor Manette falls ill again.

2 1 wedding 2 sound 3 prison 4 rude 5 pleasure 6 sadly 7 hopeless 8 kind 9 contentedly

3 Various answers are possible.

4a 4b Various answers are possible.

5 1 A considered 2 C least 3 B became 4 A include 5 A landmarks 6 A nearby 7 D wide 8 C network

6 Various answers are possible.

7a Various answers are possible.

7b 1 Sydney Carton talks to Charles after he and Lucie come back from their honeymoon. T
2 Sydney Carton wants Charles and himself to be friends. T
3 Charles says something unkind about Carton. T
4 Lucie thinks that Carton is much nicer than he seems. T
5 Charles doesn't like Carton at all. F
6 Charles promises always to remember something that Lucie has said. T

pp 76-79

1 1 Why was Lucie so silent at dinner after Charles had spoken about Sydney?
A She was very angry.
B She was thinking about something.
C She disliked talking about other people.
D She thought her husband was irresponsible.
2 What did Dickens mean by 'Lucie listened to the footsteps of the years'?
A Lucie was very imaginative.
B Her father often walked around during the day.
C Lucie was getting older and the echo of footsteps is a theme in the book.
D Lucie was worrying about the future.
3 How did Dickens describe the beginning of the revolution in France?
A Like a great storm and a terrible ocean rising.
B Like an echo in the distance.
C Like a normal July evening.
D Like any other historical event.
4 Why wouldn't the footsteps be easy to clean this time?
A This time, there were too many footsteps.
B People were too busy with the revolution.
C The marks would last because they were blood, not wine.
D People were too angry to clean them.
5 Why wasn't Madame Defarge knitting today?
A There were too many people in Defarge's café.
B Her husband was making a speech to the patriots.
C She had never been to the Bastille before.
D She was preparing to fight with the other patriots.

2a

Noun	Verb	Adjective(s)
dread	DREAD	DREADFUL
CARE	care	CARING/CAREFUL/CARELESS
STRENGTH	strengthen	STRONG
SLEEP	sleep	ASLEEP/SLEEPY/SLEEPLESS
WIDTH	widen	WIDE
blood	BLEED	BLOODY/BLOODLESS
misery	----	MISERABLE

2b SUGGESTED ANSWERS
1 It was late and the villagers were all asleep.
2 They left bloody footsteps all through Saint Antoine.
3 The gates of the Bastille were very strong.
4 Charles thought Lucie was a very caring woman.
5 There were long queues in the miserable bakers' shops.
6 Dickens compares the beginning of the revolution to 'a dreadful sea'.

3 Active and Passive.
Today, in France there (1) was (be) confusion about the situation at the terrible prison called the Bastille. Patriots attacked the towers and the gates (2) were broken down (break down) after about four hours' fighting. A white handkerchief (3) was waved (wave) from one of the towers and the patriots knew they (4) had won (win).
The prisoners in the Bastille (5) were released (release) and the Governor of the Bastille (6) was taken (take) to the Hôtel de Ville, where he (7) was executed (execute) by the mob. Seven guards from the prison (8) were killed (kill) and seven prisoners (9) were carried (carry) through the streets of Paris. No-one knows where this (10) will end (end).
4a 4b Various answers are possible.
5 Various answers are possible.
6 1 rock stone earth grass
Various answers are possible.
2 knife gun belt sword
Various answers are possible.
3 anxious threatening worried concerned
Various answers are possible.
4 rope wood chain string
Various answers are possible.
5 fountain ocean river sea
Various answers are possible.
7a 7b Various answers are possible.

pp 88-91

1

1 A Mr Lorry	7 D Monsieur Defarge
2 C Charles Darnay	8 D Monsieur Defarge
3 B Jerry Cruncher	9 D Monsieur Defarge
4 C Charles Darnay	10 C Charles Darnay
5 C Charles Darnay	11 C Charles Darnay
6 C Charles Darnay	12 C Charles Darnay

2 1 Dr Manette.
2 To help Gabelle and the other family servants.
3 Ghosts.
4 Because people didn't leave the prisons.
3 La Force was (1) one of the many prisons in Paris. By the time of the French Revolution, it had only been a prison (2) for about ten years, having previously been a private house. There were two prisons in the building, one for debtors and one for women who (3) had been arrested. During the revolution many aristocrats and former governors were held at the prison, although most were moved to another prison, La Conciergerie before (4) their execution. Dickens writes about eleven hundred prisoners (5) being murdered by the mob in the four days that Doctor Manette was away, although it may have been more. More (6) than a hundred and fifty men and women were killed at La Force. The prison was closed in 1845 and pulled down. Visitors to Paris can (7) still see the room in La Conciergerie where Queen Marie Antoinette was held before her execution.
4a 1 If I knew the man, I would take the letter to him. TAKE
2 Charles wouldn't have gone back to Paris, if Gabelle hadn't written to him. NOT WRITE
3 If Charles had stayed in England, Lucie wouldn't have gone to Paris. NOT GO
4 If I don't speak to the governors in Paris, I won't be able to go back to London. NOT BE ABLE
5 I would leave Paris, if I had enough money. HAVE
6 He won't help you, if you are an aristocrat. BE
4b Various answers are possible.
5a 1 e 2 d 3 f 4 a 5 c 6 b
5b g the legal punishment of killing someone
h to officially accuse someone of committing a crime
i to protect someone against attack or criticism
6a 6b Various answers are possible.

7 Various answers are possible.
8a Various answers are possible.
8b 1 Who was using the grindstone?
The Patriots.
2 A woman came to see Mr Lorry at Tellson's Bank in Paris. Who?
Lucie.
3 What did the woman tell Mr Lorry?
Charles is in Paris.
4 Where is Charles at the moment?
In prison.
5 Where is Doctor Manette at the moment?
At Tellson's bank in Paris.

pp 100-103

1 Dearest Miss Jones,
I'm sorry I haven't written for so long. Doctor Manette, Lucie, little Lucie and I are here in an apartment near Tellson's bank in the centre of Paris. A very ugly man called Jerry Cruncher is looking after us for Mr Lorry.
You probably already know that Charles Darnay has been in prison in La Force for more than a year! He came to France to help his family's servants and now he needs help himself. Doctor Manette is doing very well, he is a well-respected doctor in Paris.
Charles has not yet been tried in court, we expect this to happen at any time and we are afraid that the court could send him to be executed.
I'll write again as soon as I can,
Your friend,
Miss Pross
2 1 placed 2 worrying 3 considering 4 rising 5 rushed 6 terrible
3 1 Charles went to France in spite of the danger.
ALTHOUGH
Charles went to France although it was dangerous.
2 She won't be able to get there, if she doesn't leave early.
UNLESS
She won't be able to get there unless she leaves early.
3 'Why did she come back to Paris?'
SHE
He asked why she had come back to Paris.
4 'Where's the prison?'
WONDERED
She wondered where the prison was.
5 The patriots are asking him questions at the moment.
INTERVIEWED
He is being interviewed by the patriots at the moment.
6 She started to visit him a year ago.
VISITING
She has been visiting him for a year.
7 Why did you permit him to come to Paris?
LET
Why did you let him come to Paris?
8 I've never seen such a bad thing.
EVER
This is the worst thing I have ever seen.
9 'They're killing the prisoners at La Force.'
BEING
The prisoners at La Force are being killed.
4a 1 Lucie 2 Dr Manette 3 Monsieur Defarge 4 Madame Defarge
5 The president of the jury 6 Charles Darnay 7 Dr Manette
4b Various answers are possible.

5 1 Doctor Manette was proud of his actions.
2 Bread was expensive and people were hungry.
3 The streets of the city were polluted.
4 Doctor Manette was becoming influential.
5 Lucie was always polite to the mender of roads.

6a 6b Various answers are possible.

7a Various answers are possible.

pp 114-115

1 SUGGESTED ANSWERS

1 How had Doctor Manette accused his son-in-law?
By denouncing all members of the Evrémonde family when he was in prison.
2 How were the twin brothers in the doctor's letter related to Charles Darnay?
They were his father and uncle.
3 What was the relationship between the poor woman in the doctor's letter and Madame Defarge?
They were sisters.
4 Why had Doctor Manette been sent to prison at the Bastille?
Because he knew the Evrémonde family's secret.
5 What did Mr Lorry think would happen to Charles Darnay?
He thought he would be executed.
6 How did Charles Darnay escape from prison?
Sydney Carton exchanged places with him.
7 Who killed Madame Defarge?
Miss Pross.
8 Why did Miss Pross go deaf?
The sound of the gun made her go deaf.
9 How did Sydney Carton feel when he went to La Guillotine?
Peaceful.

2 Various answers are possible.

3 Various answers are possible.

4 Various answers are possible.

pp 116-117

Full Name:	Charles John Huffam Dickens
Date of Birth:	February 7th 1812
Place of Birth:	Landport, Portsmouth
Parents' Names:	John and Elizabeth Dickens
Wife's Name:	Catherine Hogarth
Children:	10
Four Important Works:	*Oliver Twist, A Christmas Carol, A Tale of Two Cities, Sketches by Boz*
Date of Death:	June 9th 1870

pp 118-119

1 When did it start?
a 1775 b 1789 c 1765
2 How many colonies first declared independence?
a 51 b 25 c 13
3 Who were the colonies separating from?
a France b England c Spain
4 When did it end?
a 1783 b 1789 c 1792

pp 120-121

Various answers are possible.

pp 122-123

Various answers are possible.

pp 124

Clues Across

2 A place in the ground where you bury a dead person. (5 letters) GRAVE
4 A room in a prison. (4 letters) CELL
6 A lawyer who tries to show that a person is guilty. (10 letters) PROSECUTOR
9 The person who does this is a traitor, and the crime is ______ . (7 letters) TREASON
10 A violent and angry crowd of people. (3 letters) MOB
11 A large container for liquid. (6 letters) BARREL

Clues Down

1 A person who goes with you to protect you or look after you. (6 letters) ESCORT
3 A repetition of a sound in the air. The sound hits something and then comes back to you. (4 letters) ECHO
5 A group of people who listen to a trial and decide if a person is guilty or innocent. (4 letters) JURY
7 You do this when you make food or drink go from your mouth into your stomach. (7 letters) SWALLOW
8 To put someone's name onto an official list. Also the list itself. (8 letters) REGISTER

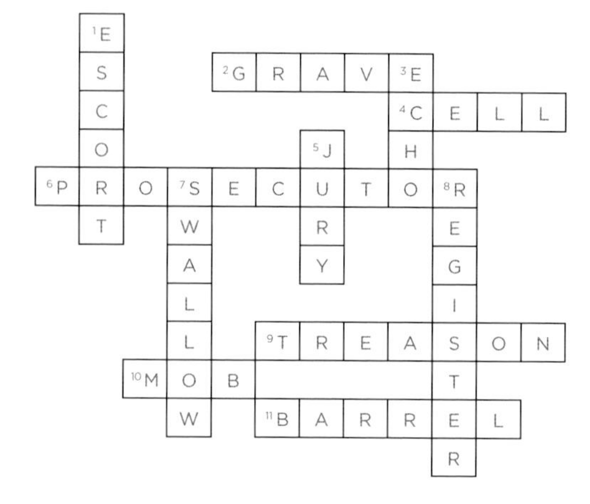

Read for Pleasure: *A Tale of Two Cities* 雙城記

作　　者：Charles Dickens
改　　寫：Janet Borsbey and Ruth Swan
繪　　畫：Giacomo Garelli
照　　片：ELI Archive and Wikimedia Commons
責任編輯：仇茵晴
封面設計：丁意
出　　版：商務印書館（香港）有限公司
香港筲箕灣耀興道 3 號東滙廣場 8 樓
http://www.commercialpress.com.hk
發　　行：香港聯合書刊物流有限公司
香港新界大埔汀麗路 36 號中華商務印刷大廈 3 字樓
印　　刷：中華商務彩色印刷有限公司
香港新界大埔汀麗路 36 號中華商務印刷大廈 14 字樓
版　　次：2017 年 4 月第 1 版第 1 次印刷

ISBN 978 962 07 0481 9
Printed in Hong Kong